PRAISE FOR

## *The Page Turner*

"Represents something of a rediscovery of the methods and ambitions of *Family Dancing* ... Indeed it shimmers with the magical talent that first announced itself a decade and a half ago."
— Michiko Kakutani, *New York Times*

"With his customary evocative prose and a lyrical continuum of characters...Leavitt strikes a note of understanding — of how parents love their children and how our hearts sometimes lead us astray."
— *Los Angeles Advocate*

"A perfectly enjoyable read...poignant."
— *New York Times Book Review*

"The sophisticated characters are adept and knowing...Leavitt's characters are serious people, aware of the consequences of their actions. In an era of talk-show confessionals, Leavitt creates characters of profound solemnity...Leavitt does know how to write."
— *San Francisco Chronicle*

"True to its title, *The Page Turner* is compelling; at times, it's also very moving."
— *Out Magazine*

"Absorbing from start to finish."
— *The New Yorker*

"Great reading...Its examination of the ambitions and uncertainties of its young protagonist will resonate deeply."
— *Windy City Times*

*The Page Turner*

# THE PAGE TURNER

## *A Novel*

## DAVID LEAVITT

*A Mariner Book*

HOUGHTON MIFFLIN COMPANY

*Boston    New York*

FIRST MARINER BOOKS EDITON 1999

Copyright © 1998 by David Leavitt

For information about permission to reproduce selections from
this book, write to Permissions, Houghton Mifflin Company,
215 Park Avenue South, New York, New York 10003.

*Library of Congress Cataloging-in-Publication Data*

Leavitt, David, date.
The page turner : a novel / by David Leavitt.
p.    cm.
ISBN 0-395-75285-X
ISBN 0-395-95787-7 (pbk.)
I. Title.
PS3562.E2618P34    1998
813'.54—dc21        97-44864    CIP

Book design by Anne Chalmers
Typeface: Granjon (Adobe PostScript™)

Printed in the United States of America

QUM 10 9 8 7 6 5 4 3 2 1

*For Mark Mitchell*

I owe much of what I know about Rome — and especially about the old Pasquino Theater — to Louis Inturrissi (1941–1997), into whose lap a cat once fell from the sky.

—D.L.

Why can't people have what they want? The things were there to content everybody; yet everybody has the wrong thing.

—Ford Madox Ford, *The Good Soldier*

# AN EAR WORM

# 1

"PAUL! Let me fix your tie!"

All at once his mother was on him, her hands at his throat.

"Mother, please, my tie's all right —"

"Let me just tighten the knot, honey, you don't want to have a loose knot for your debut —"

"It's not my debut."

"When my son sits up on a stage in front of two thousand people, I consider it a debut. There, much better."

She stepped back slightly, smoothed his lapels with long fingers. Even so, her face was close enough to kiss: he could see her crow's-feet under make-up, smell the cola-like sweetness of her lipstick, the Wrigley's on her breath.

"That's good enough, Mother."

"Just one little adjustment —"

"I said it was good enough!"

Writhing away from her, Paul hurried across the wings, to where Mr. Mansourian, the impresario, awaited him.

"Well, well, well," said Mr. Mansourian, "if you're not the best-dressed page turner I've ever seen. Come on, I'll introduce you to Kennington."

"Good luck, sweetheart!" Pamela called almost mournfully. She waved at Paul, a tissue balled in her fist. "Break a leg! I'll see you after the concert."

He didn't answer. He was out of earshot, out of the wings, beyond which the hum of the settling audience was becoming audible.

Mr. Mansourian led him up steep stairways and along anti-septic corridors, to a dressing room at the door to which he knocked three times with sharp authority.

"Come in!"

They went. In front of mirrors Richard Kennington, the famous pianist, sat on a plastic chair, bow tie slack around his throat. He was drinking coffee. Isidore Gerstler, the famous cellist, was eating a cinnamon-frosted doughnut out of a box. Maria Luisa Strauss, the famous violinist, was stubbing out a cigarette in an ashtray already overflowing with red-tipped butts. Her perfume, capacious and spicy, suggested harems. Yet the room had no softness, no Persian carpets. Instead it was all lightbulbs that brightened the musicians' faces to a yellowish intensity.

"Good evening, folks," Mr. Mansourian said, shutting the door firmly. "Richard, I'd like you to meet Paul Porterfield, your page turner."

Haltingly Kennington revolved in his seat. He had dark, flat hair, short sideburns, eyes the color of cherry wood. Fine ridges scored his face, which was slightly weather-beaten: not old-looking exactly, just older-looking than the pictures on his CDs suggested. As it happened, Paul owned all eight of Ken-nington's CDs.

Kennington smiled. "Pleased to meet you, Paul Porter-field," he said, holding out his hand.

"Thank you, sir," Paul answered, and accepted the hand with caution; after all, he'd never had the opportunity to touch anything so precious before. Yet it did not feel different from an ordinary hand, he reflected. Nor did anything in Kennington's handshake transmit to Paul the magic that happened when he sat down in front of a piano.

"This is an honor for me," Paul went on. "I've always been a great admirer of yours."

"Very kind of you to say so. And may I introduce my cohorts?"

Isidore Gerstler, still involved with his doughnut, only waved. But Maria Luisa Strauss winked at Paul, shook out her long black hair, played with the gold ankh that hung between her freckled breasts. "I've never seen such a well-dressed page turner," she said.

"So what are you working on, Paul?"

"*Kreisleriana* right now. My teacher's Olga Novotna, by the way. She said to send you her regards. And on my own, Webern. Miss Novotna doesn't approve of Webern, so —"

"Old Olga Higginbotham! Isn't she dead yet?" Isidore Gerstler interrupted.

"No sir, she's not."

"Kessler wrote the Second Symphony for her," said Maria Luisa Strauss. "*She* is O."

"I never understood why she changed her name," Kennington said. "Isn't an American name good enough? Well, we should go over the program. Pull up a chair."

Paul did. Brown circles stained the laminated surface of the table, which was empty except for a stack of scores, an eyeglass case, and a plastic bag that appeared to contain knitting.

Kennington opened the first of the scores. "So, we start with the Tchaikovsky —"

"A wonderful choice, sir, if I might say so."

"I'm glad you approve. Oh, and we take the standard cut in the variations."

"Fine."

"Then after the interval, the *Archduke*. No problems there. And if the audience behaves and we decide to do an encore, it'll be the andante from the Schubert B-flat. I presume you're familiar with the Schubert B-flat —"

"I own your 1983 recording of it with DeLaria and Miss Strauss."

Miss Strauss smiled.

"Well, you've clearly done your homework," Kennington said. "It isn't often that I get such a gung-ho page turner. In Ravenna once I had an old lady called — if you can believe it — Signora Mozzarella. Remember, Joseph? Charming but palsied."

"Signora Mozzarella is legendary in the land of Dante," Mr. Mansourian observed.

"Page turning is an art in its way, I suppose," Kennington went on. Then, taking a sip from his coffee cup, he abandoned — to Paul's lasting regret — this fascinating train of thought. "Well, I guess I'm ready. Tushi, you ready?"

"Yes, Richard."

"Izzy, you ready?"

"Yes, Richard."

"Has everybody gone?" Mr. Mansourian asked.

"Oops. Thanks for reminding me." Wiping cinnamon from his fingers, Izzy hurried into the bathroom. He didn't close the door.

An unzipping presently sounded, followed by the virile sound of flowing urine.

"Oh, please!" Mr. Mansourian clapped a hand against his forehead. "Folks, need I remind you there's a lady present?"

"Hey, Izzy, save some for me!" Kennington shouted. "I'm thirsty!"

Tushi rolled her eyes and blew a little kiss at Paul, who blushed.

"You've got to excuse us," Izzy said, zipping up. "After a few weeks on the road, we get punchy."

"Don't worry," Paul said. "I'm sure when I start my performing career, I'll get punchy too."

"Well, let's get a move on, then," Mr. Mansourian said, and opened the door.

"Good-bye," Paul said.

"Good-bye," Kennington said.

Paul followed Mr. Mansourian into the corridor.

Paul, who was just eighteen, had never turned pages before. Oh, certainly, he'd wanted to; indeed, had hinted both to Miss Novotna and Mr. Wang, his high school music teacher, how grateful he'd be for the opportunity. Nothing had happened, however, until Judith Schmidt, the musicology Ph.D. candidate at Stanford who usually took the job, decided at the last minute to attend a Shostakovich conference in Arizona. A gap opened up, one that Paul, to his delight, was asked to fill: thus houselights, backstage, the opening in the curtain through which he now glimpsed the immense Steinway, throbbing before a slice of unsettled audience.

Beside him, Mr. Mansourian was giving advice. "Just have a good time out there," he was saying. "Only be sure not to turn two pages by mistake. Richard slapped a page turner for that once."

"Don't worry. I've been practicing with my mother."

"Ah, your mother. I imagine she's taken her seat."

"I hope so."

Mr. Mansourian placed his hand on Paul's shoulder in what might have been a paternalistic gesture.

"So what are your plans, son? Hoping to make a career of it?"

"Not hoping. Intending."

"You must be very good indeed."

"Miss Novotna says I'm the most promising pupil she's had in years."

Mr. Mansourian, who had heard this kind of thing before, suppressed a smile. "Then I guess it'll be the C track," he said. "Conservatory, competitions, concerts. Yes, I can see it all.

From the Cliburn to Carnegie Hall, from Carnegie Hall to an exclusive contract —"

"That's jumping ahead of things a bit," Paul interrupted. "But I do intend to go to Juilliard, if I'm accepted."

Mr. Mansourian slipped a business card into Paul's breast pocket. "Keep this," he said. "Come play for me if you like. I've got a piano in my suite at the Clift."

"Yes, sir. Thank you, sir."

"Or we could have a drink." His stare suddenly grew cautious. "That is, if you're old enough to drink."

"Not legally."

"A Coke then," Mr. Mansourian threw out, and swallowed so hard Paul could see his Adam's apple bob.

Out in the auditorium, Paul's mother had indeed taken her place, in row twenty-two of the orchestra. Left of the aisle: Paul had told her that real music people always sit left of the aisle, so they can see the pianist's hands. Having draped her coat over the seat in front of hers, she was now scanning her program with a red-lacquered fingernail.

"No, it doesn't mention him anywhere," she said to Clayton Moss, who, along with his wife, Diane, had escorted her to the concert.

"I don't think it's customary," Clayton said. "I mean, I've never *seen* a page turner listed in the program. Diane, have you ever seen a page turner listed in the program?"

"Not that I recall." Diane was rummaging in her purse. "Anyone care for gum?"

"Did you realize that Kennington made his debut when he was fourteen? Fourteen! And put out his first record when he was sixteen!" said Clayton.

"But it's ridiculous! No thanks. I mean, they list all sorts of people — hall manager, stage manager. Why, the page turner's much more important than any of them. The pianist *needs* the page turner."

"Personally, I couldn't agree with you more," Diane said. "Personally, if it were Teddy up there, I'd be livid."

"Fourteen years old, and on a concert stage," Clayton said. "I wonder if that's right, in the end. If it damages a kid."

Pamela was thinking she might write a letter. She had written a letter the year before, when Paul had been disqualified from the youth concerto competition . . . not that it had done any good. No one cared what a mother had to say.

Pushing a fringe of hair from her eyes, she snapped open the black purse that rested on her lap. An odor of L'Air du Temps wafted from the aperture. Extracting a tissue, she dabbed at her lips.

"Sure you don't want some gum?" Diane asked. "A caramel? Cough drop?"

"Probably you think I'm just being silly. No thanks. But what can I do? I'm so proud of him. I mean, he's good, *really* good. I know you haven't heard him, Clayton. Still —"

"I've always said, if there's one thing I admire about Paul Porterfield, it's his stick-to-itiveness," Clayton said. "Especially when you consider most of these kids, with their Internet and who knows what. But Paul! Now there's a horse of a different color. I always tell Diane, that boy knows what he wants. He's disciplined, ambitious. He could be the next Van Cliburn."

"By the way, is Paul going to the Optimists' Club awards dinner this year?" Diane asked. "Teddy went last year and loved it."

"No, he's not," Pamela said frostily, and fixed her gaze on the empty stage. Optimists' Club indeed. It sorrowed her to have to keep company with people like the Mosses, who showed such little insight into the creative mind. Whereas Pamela, though possessing no creative talents of her own, at least recognized genius when she saw it; indeed, had recognized it the first time she'd heard Paul tap out a tune on the piano, the week before his fifth birthday. Even then, he'd been grasping for euphony.

She rubbed her eyes, tried to block out the fresh, intrusive memory of Diane's voice. She didn't like having to go to concerts with the Mosses, but there it was. She was not one to do things alone, and Kelso had refused. "So what if he's page-turning?" he'd said. "When he plays, I'll go." Kelso, in her view, was unforgivable, and yet his absence at least afforded her the relief of not having to worry about his falling asleep.

An enormous man with a shiny bald head now made his way to the seat in front of Pamela's. He looked at her coat, his ticket, her.

"Madame, is this yours?" he asked, indicating the coat.

"Oh, is that *your* seat? Sorry." She gathered it up.

Snorting, the man sat down. Immediately the back of his immense head supplanted the piano. In that unfortunate way of bald men, he'd grown what few hairs he had very long, then brushed them forward over his scalp.

Now if Clayton were a gentleman, she thought, he'd offer to trade places with her. But clearly Clayton wasn't a gentleman because he didn't do anything. Which was typical. Nothing ever worked out the way she hoped. Even so, she wouldn't have dreamed of *asking* Clayton to change places with her, both because she was too proud and because in truth she rather relished the prospect of a little public suffering.

The hall lights dimmed. Immediately the buzz of audience chatter shrank to a whisper.

"It's starting!" Pamela said to Clayton, and craned her neck to see. Aside from the piano and Kennington's bench, the stage's only occupants were three chairs and two music stands. Presently, no one joined them. Had the dimming been a false alarm? The collective held breath of the audience tautened as the seconds passed. It was as if an immense bubble were forming over the auditorium. Then some people stepped onto the stage. Applause popped the bubble, applause that had as much to do with relief as enthusiasm. The cellist came first, chubby and pink, his face framed by coarse curls. Next followed the violinist, a dark woman in a black skirt and leotard. When she bowed, her body went limp like a rag doll, her hair, as lustrous as the piano itself, fell forward and nearly brushed the floor.

Finally there was the pianist. A younger man than Pamela

had expected, he appeared distracted, as if it were just dawning on him that he was in a public place. Pushing through the applause as if it were foliage, he moved to his bench. Paul, trailing, took the chair at the piano's left, then settled the score on the desk.

While the cellist and the violinist opened their own music, the pianist whispered something to Paul, in response to which he took off his watch and stuffed it into his breast pocket.

"Look at him!" Pamela nudged Clayton with her elbow. "Oh, but his tie! He must have fiddled with it."

"It's fine, Pammy."

The bald man turned. "Ssh!" he said, and Pamela colored. He opened a score over his lap.

Closing his eyes, the pianist clasped his hands for a few seconds, as if in prayer, then, when the theater was silent, nodded to his partners, who nodded back.

They began to play. As for Pamela, very quietly she scooted forward and pressed her knee against the back of the bald man's seat. He raised his head. A vein pulsed behind his ear. Serves him right, she thought, folding up her coat.

It was toward the end of the Tchaikovsky (and of course it had to be Tchaikovsky) that Kennington, much to his chagrin and surprise, began to become aware of Paul; that is to say, aware of him as more than just a black arm that shot forward every time he neared the end of a page, held the corner steady between thumb and forefinger, and in response to the subtlest of nods, with sparrowlike swiftness, turned it. Invisibility is an

asset in any page turner: on stage, he must efface his presence
as much as possible, make it seem as if the sheets are flipping
of their own accord. And in terms of unobtrusiveness, Paul
was faultless. He never turned a page too late or too early,
never sniffled or shook his leg. Yes, the watch had been a
mistake, but this Kennington forgave, attributing it to inex-
perience. In any event Paul had taken it off as soon as he
was asked to do so. And still, even without the watch, Ken-
nington found himself growing conscious of Paul, of his
slightly parted legs, the folds of black wool at his crotch, the
white shirting where his jacket fell open; indeed, so distracted
was he that when the Tchaikovsky ended, and the boy, well
versed in the ways of page turners, gathered up the scores and
stood aside for him to pass, Kennington hurried backstage
and headed immediately for the water cooler. Even at this
distance, Paul's heavy, almost medicinal odor prickled in his
throat.

When the houselights came up, he asked if there was some-
place he could go by himself. He had a headache, he said. The
stage manager led him to an empty dressing room, where he
sat before a scratched and battered table, the lights off, his
fingers on his temples. Unlike Izzy Gerstler, he was not an
experienced libertine; nor was it his habit to be driven to
dementia by page turners. And yet something about Paul's
nervous meticulousness, his good manners, the razor-sharp
part in his hair, alarmed Kennington. He could not say why,
exactly. Perhaps it was the degree to which Paul seemed an
echo of himself, years earlier. (As a boy, making his first

*tournée* of Europe, he too must have given off that musk of animal discomfort.) Also the tingle of unexpressed need that now clung to Kennington's suit, picked up like static electricity from a wall socket.

A knock sounded. "Five minutes!" the stage manager called, and Kennington stumbled onto his feet. To his embarrassment he had an erection. He closed his eyes, tried to will it away, for he couldn't very well walk out on stage like that. And yet despite his efforts to fill his mind only with the *Archduke,* an image of Paul on all fours, with his shorts around his knees, materialized insistently on the insides of his eyelids. On the insides of his eyelids he was stroking the arched behind, the line of pale hairs that ran from the small of the back into the cleft between the buttocks. And Paul was begging him, he was saying, "Please, sir. Please." This wasn't in itself unusual. In fantasy at least, Kennington liked being begged. He liked withholding before satisfying. It was all rather like a curtain call.

No, the thing that unnerved him was that the fantasy seemed to be having him rather than the other way around.

Another knock. "Mr. Kennington?"

"Okay," he said, and pulling himself together, headed downstairs. In the wings Paul stood where he had left him, apparently not having moved for the entire length of the interval. "Feeling all right, sir?" he asked, his cheeks pink, gazing at Kennington with horrible sincerity.

"Better now."

They returned to the stage. In the orchestra the last stragglers hurried to their seats, applauding even as they ran. Opening the score, Paul tried not to look at the backs of the bowing players, the lights, the blur of human pandemonium in the midst of which, somewhere, his mother sat, probably waving at him. (It was embarrassing even to contemplate.)

At last Tushi, arranged in her chair, nodded to Kennington. The audience quieted, and the *Archduke* began.

It is the rare privilege of a page turner to hear a pianist almost as he hears himself: to hear his humming, the occasional grunts that escape through his teeth, the dull clack of his nails against the keys. And not only hear, but see; study. As Paul was learning, Kennington didn't move a lot when he performed, didn't lunge or writhe on the bench, or drape himself over the keyboard in an attitude of sublime transfiguration. Instead his face remained impassive, even expressionless. He kept his lips together, his back straight, supple. And those hands! Earlier, they had seemed unremarkable to Paul, but now, in the throes of *doing,* they revealed their rarity. Precision and unity, that was the formula, each note offered with an eloquence that somehow never distracted from the larger narrative in which it was bound. His hands were themselves a kind of music.

Forty minutes later, when the trio ended and the applause began, Paul obediently picked up the score and followed the musicians off the stage. Izzy Gerstler was wiping his mouth with a wrinkled handkerchief.

"So what say we let the blue hairs have a chance to clear out, then give them the Schubert?" he asked.

"Fine," Tushi said. "Richard, you up for it?"

"What? Oh, sure."

They did not move. From the upper tiers the music students stomped rhythmically, insistent that the musicians should now play their appointed roles in that approach-avoidance ritual known as the encore — an insistence they knew better than to oblige too quickly. After all, a certain coquettishness is expected from great artists. Not to keep your public waiting would spoil the game.

Finally, in wordless agreement, the trio filed out onto the stage, bowed, filed back. In row twenty-two Pamela Porterfield rose to her feet.

"Bravo!" she shouted.

No one else was standing.

Embarrassed, she sat down again.

"Diane, have you got any aspirin?"

"Sure thing, honey."

"You all right, Pammy?" Clayton asked.

"Oh, I'm fine. I just have this crick in my neck from stretching to see over that man's head. Thanks." She rubbed her left shoulder. "You were lucky, Clayton. You didn't have anyone in front of you."

Instead of answering, Clayton clapped. Diane put on her coat. Already most of the subscription holders were hurrying out, eager to be first in line at the coat check or the valet parking. Idiots, Pamela thought (swallowing the aspirin), the kind of people who unwrap hard candy during the slow movement, or applaud before the end, or talk. Why, once she and Paul had sat next to a man who'd actually brought along a transistor radio to a recital, so he could listen to the World Series. The management had had to be summoned.

"So what'd you think?" Diane asked. In the narrow aisle she was already buttoned up, purse in hand.

"I liked the Beethoven better than the Tchaikovsky," Clayton said.

"Really? I liked the Tchaikovsky better than the Beethoven."

"How about you, Pammy? Which one did you like better?"

Pamela, still seated, said nothing, as the trio, wearing expressions of reluctance and indulgence, stepped back onto the stage. This time Kennington led. They carried instruments, music. Those people who happened to be in the aisles grabbed whatever empty seat was closest. Chatter and applause ceased utterly, as if a vacuum had sucked away sound.

The Mosses, looking disappointed, sat down again.

Almost offhandedly, Kennington struck the first chord of the Schubert. It is a piece that brings to mind the moment of departure at a train station; that makes the fingers stretch to touch a last time; that makes you think, yes, the life of sensation, and no other. Indeed, Kennington's playing of it transfixed Paul's attention to such a degree that at one point he nearly forgot to turn the page. But fortunately he caught himself, and from then on he made certain to keep his eyes on the score instead of the keyboard.

The andante lasted a little more than eight minutes, after

which the musicians got up, bowed again, and left the stage. Ritual demanded further curtain calls, further stomping for a second encore that was not forthcoming: with the exception of Izzy, who could have played all night, they were too tired.

"That's it!" the stage manager shouted as the houselights went up. Roars of disappointment sounded from the upper balconies.

People left.

In a corner of the wings, meanwhile, Kennington was drinking water from a cooler: cup after cup, gulp after gulp.

Very quietly Paul approached him.

"Sir?" he asked, holding out his hand.

"Yes?"

"I'm sorry to interrupt you. I just want to say that you played splendidly tonight."

"Thank you."

"I'll never forget it, not for the rest of my life. Sorry about the watch, by the way."

"Oh, that was no problem."

"Also, I realize that I nearly missed one turn during the encore."

"It was nothing. From my point of view you were perfect. Flawless, even."

"I appreciate that, sir, even if it isn't true."

"Please don't call me sir. I'm not that old. I'm not your grandfather."

"But I didn't say it because I thought you were old. I said it because I think you're great."

"Well, that's a little better, I suppose." Filling his cup again, Kennington looked at Paul, who with a kind of studied obduracy was refusing to meet his eye, fixing his attention instead on the men in overalls who were moving the piano off the stage.

"So do you live here in San Francisco?" he asked after a moment.

"In Menlo Park, actually. That's down the peninsula. But I was born in Boston." Paul smiled. "You're from Florida, aren't you?"

"Yes, I am."

"I only mention it because I have aunts in Florida. In Hallandale."

"That's the other end of the state from me. Holmbury is near the Georgia border."

"I know where it is. I looked it up in the atlas. I'd like to go to Holmbury some day and pay my regards to Clara Aitken."

"How do you know about Clara Aitken?"

"Judging from what you said in that interview in the November 1986 issue of *Gramophone,* she must have been quite a teacher." He blushed.

Kennington laughed. "It sounds like you know more about me than I know about myself."

"What can I say? You're a role model to me, sir — I mean, Mr. Kennington."

"Richard."

"Richard." Paul grimaced, blushed.

"There, that wasn't so bad, was it? And anyway, wouldn't you agree that it's much more pleasant to be called by your own name?"

Paul seemed to consider the question seriously. Then he said, "Well, I'd better be going. Good luck with the rest of your tour. And thank you. Again."

"Thank *you*, Paul," Kennington answered; yet he did not take the hand Paul held out. Instead he stepped closer. "In a way, I'm sorry you have to go."

"Why?"

"Well, I was thinking we could have a drink together, or . . ."

Paul's eyes widened. "A drink? But people must be taking you out!"

"No, no one's taking me out."

"But I came with my mother, and I haven't got a ride home. I couldn't —"

"That's fine."

"Not that I don't want to. Of course I want to . . . only how would I —"

"Paul!"

"Well, you could take a taxi. I'd be glad to —"

He turned. His mother was striding toward them, flanked by the Mosses.

Instantly Kennington drew back, drew away.

"Darling, I'm so proud of you!" Pamela said, filling the air with her scent of cola and perfume. "You were wonderful!"

"Mom, please —"

He looked over her head for Kennington. From where he'd stood Diane Moss pulled a camera from her purse.

"Say cheese!"

"Cheese!" Pamela said.

A flash went off. For a moment its reddening waves blinded Paul, who blinked, signaled with his arm. "Wait!" he almost called. But the darkness had picked up Kennington, and carried him away.

He still held the music. What was he supposed to do with the music?

"Honey, are you all right?" his mother asked.

"Fine," he said. "Excuse me, will you?" And he went off to ask the stage manager where to leave the scores.

# 2

MISS OLGA NOVOTNA (née Higginbotham), eighty-six
years old with flame red hair, liked to claim she'd been re-
sponsible for Kennington's career. "This was almost twenty-
five years ago," she told Paul as they drank tea in her apart-
ment on Russian Hill. "I'd been asked to serve on the jury of
the Chopin, and Kennington was one of the competitors.
He couldn't have been much older than you are now. And
when he performed — well, I was overwhelmed. It was as if
Chopin had been waiting for this young man to be born. So
you can imagine my astonishment when a few hours later, still
aglow from his performance, I found that he had failed to
make the semifinals." She raised a jeweled hand to her neck.
"My back went up, Paul. I tell you, my back went up."

"What did you do?"

"I said to my fellow jurors, if you eliminate Richard Ken-
nington, you eliminate me. I resign from this jury."

"And you walked out?"

"I never judged the Chopin again. Of course they laughed
at me. Oh, they regretted it later, when he got the contract,
and was famous overnight. Vindication is sweet, my dear!
Never forget it."

"Who won that year?"

Miss Novotna shrugged. "Who remembers? No one that matters. Take it as a lesson, Paul. Mediocrity rewards its own, but talent will always out. Now play *Bydlo,* and remember, hard at first, then soar, as if the cart is rising into the heavens."

Paul played. In his mind he was Kennington — the young Kennington, from his first album cover — losing the Chopin. For weeks now, ever since his page-turning debut, he'd been trying to learn as much about Kennington (Richard!) as he could. Unfortunately information proved scarce. All he knew was what he'd gleaned from magazines and liner notes: that Kennington had grown up in Florida (teacher Clara Aitken, herself a pupil of Dohnányi); that he'd started performing at fourteen, made his first recording at sixteen ("one of the few piano prodigies," *Gramophone* magazine said, "to survive the difficult transition from *wunderkind* to superstar"); that he lived (alone) in New York.

When his lesson ended, Paul gave Miss Novotna a rose that he'd brought in his satchel. "And now you are off to Italy," she said. "Oh, my dear, how I envy you."

"I'll send you a postcard from every city I go to."

"Italy! I remember it as if it were yesterday. The Pergola, the San Carlo." She shook her aristocratic old head. "Well, you are young, and you deserve it — and yet age has its pleasures too. Remember that as you make your way. I went through it all with Kessler. First they crown you a young king, and then you turn thirty and find you can do no right with them, and then when years have passed of struggle and disappointment, suddenly you find yourself an old man, and the crown on your head again. Horowitz went through it. Kennington may be going through it now."

Paul became brave. "Tell me more about Kessler," he said.

She lifted her hands in a gesture of questioning. "What's there to tell? The music says more. That was why I stopped playing. Because he needed me in order to write. And if I hadn't, you realize, Paul, there would have been no Second Symphony. There would have been no Third Symphony." She folded her white arms atop the table. "The feminists will say I had no business to do it, and I'm sure in principle they're right. And yet a world without that music . . . well, it simply can't be imagined, can it? Whereas what contribution *I* might have made . . ." She laughed bitterly.

"But you were a great pianist."

"No, no. I might have been . . ." She closed her eyes. "Every great artist is a vampire, Paul. Remember that. They will suck you dry."

"What an amazing life you've had, Miss Novotna. It's like a novel."

"I often thought of writing one. And now Kessler's biographer sends me nagging little letters every other week. What was Kessler's opinion of York Bowen, Miss Novotna? Do you happen to have the program from the 1961 Maggio Musicale, Miss Novotna? Is it true that Kessler left sketches for an opera based on *The Good Soldier,* Miss Novotna? Oh, she bores me!

But speaking of boredom, this old lady has probably tired you enough for one day. Now go, go to Rome." And she patted him on the behind.

"Thank you. Good-bye."

"Say *ciao* to the Campidoglio from an old friend," she called, while the surly-looking maid held the door open.

Out on the street, the sun warmed the top of Paul's head. He tried to absorb Miss Novotna's final advice for future use and contemplation; and yet the troubles of thirty can mean little to one for whom twenty is still an unimaginable horizon. Nor can the fate of a woman who gave up her career for love of someone greater seem very real to a boy who has never touched, never kissed, another body.

Well, that's that, he thought, as he climbed on the bus to the train station. The last piano lesson. The last bus ride home from a piano lesson. Very possibly the last time he'd see his old teacher, whom he loved dearly. At the thought of her dying, a quiver of loss registered in his bones. His heart broke a little. It was interesting. Though Paul possessed the full complement of emotions, most of them were as yet untested. Now, in a controlled way, he flexed the muscles of grief; imagined himself attractively mournful at Miss Novotna's funeral; planned the oration he'd deliver, the music he'd play: Schumann, of course; and maybe that Brahms intermezzo she loved so much . . .

At the station, as was his ritual, he bought a candy bar. Then he threw it away uneaten because candy bars were one of the desperate consolations of his adolescence, and his adolescence, which he had loathed, was as of today officially over. How interminable they had seemed to him, those years, a kind of endless Sunday afternoon of the soul, every shop locked and shuttered! Now he could luxuriate in the contemplation of past miseries from afar. He could bask in that calm that descends when one thing is over, the next has yet to begin, all is potential and thus harmless; yes, for the moment Paul sits still and tilting, a rider atop a stopped Ferris wheel below whom the world spreads out its unexpected symmetries. That was then, it says. This is next. There is no now.

On the train he got hungry, and regretted having thrown away the candy bar. It seemed extraordinary to him that the flight to Rome left in less than twenty-four hours, that in twenty-four hours he'd be in the air. And how remote this landscape of tract houses and chain motels seemed from the imagined vantage point of the plane! Through the sooty glass of the window, the lights of the houses seemed as pregnant with imminent loss as those on Christmas trees. He looked upon them with generosity. These days he was looking upon all kinds of things with generosity that until recently he had thought base and ugly. Just a week ago, for instance, having cleaned out his locker and taken a long-rehearsed final glance at the band room, he had gotten on his bicycle and pedaled away from his high school for the last time. In the dusk sky an orange lozenge of sun melted. Knowledge of lastness made the grim architecture almost beautiful. "Yes, you are beautiful, too!" Paul said to the high school, which regarded him with bemused indifference, hardly distinguishing his presence among multitudes.

It would have been pleasant if Paul could have stayed a long time in that caesura, that bountiful sway atop the Ferris wheel. Such calm is rare in any life, and grows rarer as one gets older; in some cases it never comes at all; in Paul's case it was destined to last only the length of the train ride.

When he climbed down onto the platform, his mother's station wagon wasn't there. Several other cars waited in front of the depot. Pamela's just wasn't one of them.

He sat on the curb. How strange, he thought. She's always on time. She must be packing. Meanwhile the last of the cars took on its passenger and drove off. Paul was alone. As a child, not being picked up had been one of his animal terrors. Whenever his mother had been late to fetch him he'd sat in the school library and imagined twelve-car pileups. Now once again he imagined twelve-car pileups, in which case the trip to Italy would have to be canceled, he would have no choice but to go on living in this country of his childhood: this country which, because he was fleeing it forever, he could forgive, but which if he had to remain in it, he sensed, would never forgive him.

He shut his eyes. To that demigod that promises (falsely) to fulfill the selfish wishes of the young, he prayed that his mother might be spared until they got back from Italy.

A few minutes later, as if in answer to his prayer, headlamps bloomed in the dark. He recognized the familiar trim of her station wagon, stood up, climbed in.

"What happened?" he asked.

Pamela had on her dark glasses. She sat huddled over the steering wheel, shoulders hunched, her hair held back with a rubber band.

"Mother?"

She didn't move.

"He's not coming," she said.

"Who?"

"Your father."

"Not coming where?"

Switching off the ignition, she laid her head against the steering wheel. "God, it's just like him. Waiting until the day before a trip to spring the news."

"I don't understand. What's happened? Dad's not coming to Italy?"

"Your father is having an affair," Pamela said. "Is — has been for years. It all came out this afternoon. I had the feeling he's just been bursting to tell me. So now the plan is that you and I go off to Italy by ourselves like nothing's happened, while he and the woman shack up stateside, nice and cozy —"

For air, Paul rolled down the window.

"The bastard."

"Mom —"

"The fucking bastard."

"Don't say that!"

She beat her fists on the steering wheel.

"Mom —"

All at once she switched on the ignition, pulled fast out of the parking lot.

"Where are we going? Careful!" She had raced a yellow light.

Veering onto El Camino, she drove up to a motel, its red VACANCY sign brazen in the dark.

"Mother, we can't stay in a motel. I have to pack."

"He named the business after it," she said. "Because it was where they met on their lunch hours all those years. That's why he named the business Summit Printing. The bastard."

She started crying.

Through the windshield Paul read the words SUMMIT MOTOR LODGE in green and white neon.

He said nothing. Nothing in his experience had prepared him for this moment. Still, some instinct told him to reach out a hand and steady his mother's shoulder. She flinched it away. Probably she understood that if he wanted to comfort her, it was not for her sake at all; it was because he could not bear for her to show weakness in his proximity.

Finally she opened her purse and took out a tissue.

"Well," she said.

"What are we going to do?" Paul asked.

"What are we going to do? Go. You think I want to stick around here and watch? He's the past."

Paul shut his eyes.

She reversed out of the Summit Motor Lodge parking lot

and headed into traffic. "Yes, in the end I'll probably be relieved," she said. "In the end I'll probably decide it was for the best."

Paul stayed quiet. A few minutes later, they were pulling into the familiar driveway. "Is he here?" he asked.

She shook her head. "He won't come back until after we're gone."

They went in through the garage. Under Paul's feet, the floorboards were reticent. The doors creaked. The kitchen kept to itself, like a beaten child who fears reprisal.

Suddenly he no longer enjoyed looking forward. He simply wanted to be in the future, remembering misery, instead of in the present, remembering having looked forward to joy.

Taking a dish of sugar-free Jell-O out of the refrigerator, Pamela sat down at the kitchen table and started a crossword puzzle.

"Aren't you going to pack?" Paul said.

"In a minute," Pamela said. "Honey, you know everything about music. Composer Maurice —"

"Ravel," Paul said.

"Ravel," Pamela repeated. "Yes, that's fine. Yes, that'll fit in perfectly."

# 3

FORTY SOME ODD HOURS LATER, in his hotel room in Rome, Paul opened the letter his father had slipped inside his suitcase. "It's okay for you to hate me," Kelso concluded, "as long as it motivates you to take care of your mother. Remember, I won't always be her husband, but you'll always be her son, so make sure she doesn't do anything you'll regret."

After he'd folded the letter in eighths and stuffed it inside his jeans pocket, Paul opened the window. A soppy world confronted him, the air colorless and woolly in the damp. Nearby, in her own room, his mother slept off jet lag and grief. He himself wasn't tired at all, even though he hadn't been to bed in what felt like days. So he took his old umbrella and went out walking.

It was another long-rehearsed moment that would only come once: his first walk, alone, through the streets of Rome. And yet like most longed-for things, the Pantheon was simply there, sinking wonderfully into the mist. Inside, the rain seemed to fall in slow motion through the oculus. A camp of vagrants, complete with dogs and guitars and blankets, sheltered under the portico. He listened to the ground bass and trill of rain.

Turning left, Paul wandered down a succession of ever-narrowing streets. Churches faced him at every corner. He stepped into one of them. A congested light filtered through the old windows, clogging the vast interior with shadows. Behind a half-open door a nun ironed altar cloths.

He sat down. White candles burned in corners. All around him gloomy frescoes rose: Santa Agatha with her breasts on a plate, Santa Lucia with her eyes on a plate. Then an old woman entered the church, crossed herself, stepped into one of the confessionals. He heard her muttered litany. From under the curtain the priest's black shoe tapped a beat.

He thought, *It's not supposed to be like this;* he thought, *My mother's tragedy is not my tragedy.* After all, he had taken a lifesaving course once, and therefore knew that the greatest risk in trying to save someone is that that person will climb atop your shoulders and drown you too.

Still, he could not help remembering how in the taxi, when the driver had overcharged them, she'd said, "It's okay, Paul. One of the only pleasures I have left is wasting your father's money."

Once the rain had eased, Paul left the church and, following the signs, walked toward Piazza Navona. Soon the smell of coffee drew him into a shop with a sign that said *torrefazione.* There were no other customers. The handsome barman, redheaded and hairy-armed, was taking advantage of the lull to polish his instrument with a white cloth.

"*Prego,*" he said.

"*Un cappuccino,*" Paul said, for the first time putting into practice the Italian he had been studying in his room for weeks.

"*Va bene,*" the barman said, and slapped a saucer down onto the marble counter. His machine was an impressive piece of engineering, part plumbing and part cookware. Mosque-shaped, formed from beaten brass and steel, it had two little balconies hanging off its sides, on one of which the cup was placed to receive the coffee's slow drip. The milk he foamed with a limblike extension, from which hot blasts of steam issued.

"*Un bel cappuccino caldo,*" he repeated, depositing the cup on the saucer.

"*Grazie.*"

"*Tedesco, lei?*"

"*Americano.*"

"Where are you from?"

"California."

"Ah, California. Beautiful girls, eh?" He made a gesture in front of his chest to indicate large breasts.

Paul's face flushed in the warmth. He drank. The barman was telling him the story of his life, which was elaborate. He was from Cefalù, he said, in Sicily. In Rome he lived with his girlfriend. But now they were thinking of moving to America because she had relatives who owned a restaurant in Cincinnati. He said he liked the name of that city because it included the toast *cin-cin.* Would he like a grappa? the barman asked, and Paul said yes.

"*Sono Paolo,*" he said. They shook hands. The barman did

not offer his own name. Instead he picked up a bottle shaped like a pear and poured out a tiny glassful of clear emulsion, which he handed to Paul. "Thank you," Paul said. *"Cin-cin."* He toasted the air. The barman smiled. A thin thread of gold disappeared into his collar, Paul noticed: and what hung at the end of it? A cross, probably. Or a *corno* to ward off the evil eye.

The grappa was stronger than anything he had ever tasted. It made him purse his lips. Could the barman get into trouble for giving alcohol to someone who was underage? In America, certainly. And yet it was becoming every moment more evident that he was in another land.

After a few sips of the grappa Paul's chest felt warm, as if someone had been rubbing it with Ben-Gay.

The barman kept talking. He told a long story about a child who had fallen from a tower, but because the child's mother had had the good sense to invoke the name of San Francesco di Paola, instead of crashing down, the child had wafted gently to the earth like a leaf. Then he put his elbow on the bar, rested his cheek in his palm, and said, *"Insomma."* In sum, Paul translated mentally. *"Insomma, poi, niente."* He drew circles on the marble with his fore-finger. No language has more ways of saying nothing than Italian.

After a while Paul announced that he had to go to the bathroom. He was shivering a little. And why? Nothing had happened. And what was he expecting anyway? That the barman would follow him into the bathroom, that they would pee side by side? (The thought excited and shamed him.) But instead he just stood there and drew circles, and said, *"Insomma."* As far as Paul could tell his friendliness had neither conditions nor expectations attached to it, which surprised him. He had never before encountered friendliness for its own sake, friendliness that formed like a skin over the surface of the moment, only to break when the spoon plunged in.

Returning from the bathroom, he asked how much he owed. "One thousand five hundred," the barman said, ringing up.

"And the grappa?"

*"Niente."*

"But —"

*"Niente."*

It seemed futile to argue when faced with such an edifice of masculine will. Thanking him, Paul picked up his umbrella and left.

Outside, the rain seemed finally to have let up. Cold leftover drops fell onto his hair from balconies. Somehow he knew that back at the hotel, his mother had woken.

Ignoring the maternal tug, he kept walking. Against the wall of a brooding palazzo a beige poster drooped in the damp. He went to study it: RICHARD KENNINGTON, PIANOFORTE, it declared. CHOPIN, BRAHMS, RAVEL...

He searched for the date, saw that the concert had taken place the night before.

Suddenly a strangled sensation seized him, anguish holding exultation in its scissors grip.

"Fuck," he said. An old lady smiled. "Shit." A boy with a heavy backpack rode by on a bicycle.

Finally he said, "Nothing works out for me" (he was his mother's son), then, breathless, hurried back to the hotel. In the dim lobby an old woman sat knitting in a rocking chair, her attention fixed on a black-and-white television that chattered near the ceiling. Behind a bar, a sullen youth was wiping a plate with his apron. A signora, Valkyrian in aspect, occupied the front desk in much the same way that large countries occupy small countries during a war.

Thunder broke in the distance. The yellow lights wavered, steadied.

*"Buona sera, signorino."*

*"Buona sera."* He took his key.

Upstairs, more light escaped from under his mother's door, on which he knocked.

"Who is it?" she asked timorously.

"Paul."

She opened for him. "Oh, sweetheart, I'm so glad it's you. Where have you been? I was frightened."

"I took a walk."

He stepped into her room. The chandelier shone loudly. It was not a comforting light. In it, his mother looked suddenly very small to him, almost birdlike. And he was still young enough to be a little shocked by how much he'd outgrown her.

He sat down on the iron bed. Over its various posts and bars Pamela had draped her underwear and nylons. "I tell you, the bathroom's been a real adventure," she said. "First the hot water was on the side of the sink that the cold water was supposed to be on. And then to make things even more confusing, the cold side said 'F' and the hot side said 'C.'"

"*Caldo* and *freddo*."

"Right, and *caldo* means cold."

"No, *caldo* means hot."

"Well, anyway, it basically *was* cold. Lukewarm at most. And instead of a proper tub, there's just a showerhead on the wall and a kind of drain thing on the floor. I nearly flooded the place. And the toilet —"

Paul lay back. His posture told Pamela to shut up about the bathroom.

"So, are you hungry?" she asked instead, and looked at him cautiously, as if to gauge his emotional temperature.

Paul shrugged. "Not really. You?"

"I could eat. I mean, I *should* eat. We need to adjust to the schedule over here, and probably the best way to do it is just to pretend we're not tired when we're tired, pretend we're hungry when we're not hungry."

"You go," Paul said.

"You mean alone?"

"You eat. I'm exhausted."

Pamela frowned. "But Paul," she said. "It's our first night —"

"Mother, I just want to make one thing clear. I'm happy to be on this trip with you, I'm happy to be seeing Italy with you, only if we're going to get along, you have to give me time by myself. I'm eighteen now. I'm an adult."

"I know that, Paul. And of course the last thing I want is to burden you. But this *is* our first night, and anyway, I don't understand the money, your Italian is so good —"

"Just go downstairs and have some supper in the hotel restaurant. The waiters speak English and they'll put the charges on the bill. I have to sleep."

Reluctantly, his mother slunk off to consume her solitary meal, while Paul hurried to his own room. To get there, he had to walk down a corridor overlaid with a thinning Persian runner, across a loggia draped with flowers, up a short staircase, through a foyer with a piano, down another short staircase, through the lobby and up the main stairs to the top floor. Here there was no carpeting at all. The corridor was as narrow as a vise. Still, he liked the room, which had a sleigh bed and writing table, and reminded him of the one Van Gogh had painted in Arles. The walls were patterned with fading violets. (Or was it a pattern of faded violets?) There was even a genuine architectural oddity: a window that started halfway down the wall and ended at the floor. When the weather improved, he thought he might sit in this window, dangling his feet amid the red tiled rooftops, in the river of the world.

Having combed his hair and put on his jacket, he hurried back to the lobby. From behind the desk, the massive signora smiled at him without showing her teeth. Altogether she seemed upholstered: an upright, walking sofa.

He requested, and was given, a telephone directory, as well as a copy of the day's newspaper, on the culture page of which a review of Kennington's concert featured prominently.

Appropriating a little black phone in the corner booth, he started dialing all the five-star hotels, asking at each one for the room of Richard Kennington. "No, I'm sorry," the operators told him in their careful English, "No, there's no one here by that name," until finally, at the Bristol, the voice said, "One moment." Then there was a pause, another ring.

"Hello?"

Paul hung up. Returning to the front desk, he asked the signora how to find the Via Veneto.

He didn't know exactly why he was going, or what he'd do once he got there: only that having missed the concert, he must not miss Kennington himself.

The Bristol proved to be a very grand place indeed. The lobby had marble floors, porters, men in somber suits fussing behind inlaid wood counters.

"I'm here to see Mr. Kennington," he told the concierge.

"May I ask your name?"

"Porterfield. Paul Porterfield."

Looking slightly suspicious, the concierge picked up a telephone. "Mr. Kennington," he said in English. "There is a young man to see you. A Mr. Porterfield. Sorry? Yes? One moment."

He handed Paul the phone.

"Hello?"

"Mr. Kennington — Richard — this is Paul Porterfield. Do you remember me?"

"Who?"

"I turned pages for you a few months back in San Fran-

cisco. The chamber music concert. You played the Tchai-
kovsky trio, the *Archduke,* then as an encore —"

"Oh, yes. What are you doing in Rome?"

"I'm here with my mother on vacation. And I saw the
poster for your concert. I could kick myself! We only got in
today." He lowered his voice. "I called all over the place
looking for you. I'm amazed I found you. I wondered . . .
well, you may have forgotten, but after the concert in San
Francisco you suggested we might . . . we never had the
chance then, but now —"

Up in his room, Kennington, who had been in the midst of
writing a letter to Mr. Mansourian explaining his intention
to retire from live performance forever, brushed his hand
through his hair. Sometimes at the least expected, most pain-
ful moment, the world presents you with an opportunity for
relief.

"Give me five minutes," he said. "Then come up. Room
611."

He hung up the phone. Hurrying to his closet, he pulled on
jeans, a white oxford broadcloth shirt. He brushed his teeth,
splashed some Acqua di Parma on his neck.

Exactly five minutes later, a knock sounded on the door.
Kennington opened it.

Yes, it was the same boy. He still had his hair parted per-
fectly.

"Hello," Paul said.

"Well," Kennington said.

He held the door open, and Paul stepped through.

# 4

"HELP YOURSELF to something from the minibar," Kennington said, opening the little refrigerator under the television.

"Thank you." Paul peered inside. There were rows of miniature liquor bottles of the sort his father collected, Toblerone chocolate bars, cashew nuts.

After some consideration he chose pear nectar, while Kennington poured himself a glass of bourbon from a large bottle on the windowsill. Paul looked around. It was easily the fanciest hotel room he'd ever been in. The walls were upholstered in some sort of creamy silk fabric he would have liked to caress. Chintz curtains patterned with roses met over the windows. The dark walnut of the armoire matched that of the bedstead, which encased a big double mattress, its sheet folded over neatly in one corner. Yet what impressed Paul even more than the luxury of the room was that Kennington had thrown his things around as casually as if it were anywhere at all: a can of shaving cream on the dresser, a bruised wallet and some change on the side table, a skinny black sock draped over a chair.

They sat, Paul in the china blue armchair, Kennington on the edge of the bed.

"Well, *cin-cin,*" Paul said, and toasted.

"*Cin-cin.*"

"You're very nice to have invited me up," he continued. "Believe me, I never expected it."

"Why?"

"Well, you must have much better things to do with your time than sit here with a page turner."

"Not really."

"But what about your tour?"

"It's over. As of this morning, I'm officially on vacation."

"Still, you must know a lot of people in Rome."

"No."

Blushing, Paul scratched at the fabric of the armchair. "Boy, I almost can't believe this is happening. Maybe it's jet lag. I mean, when I walked up to that concierge, I was sweating bullets. I never in a million years imagined —"

"You are ballsy, I'll give you that. When I was your age, I never would have been brave enough —"

"Oh, but I'm not brave. Or I should say, I'd never have been brave if it hadn't been you. Only when I saw that poster, and saw that I'd missed your concert by just one night, I couldn't bear the bad timing of it, especially after what happened in San Francisco. So I decided to take my chances. I just started calling one hotel after another, only the five-star ones, of course."

Kennington stretched out his legs. "The page turner from San Francisco," he said, smiling. Then he got up and, strolling over to Paul's chair, knelt in front of him and tousled his hair.

"You know, Tushi couldn't get over how well dressed you were. Better than she was, in my opinion."

"I only dressed the way I would have expected a page turner to dress if I'd been playing."

"How old did you say you were?"

"I didn't. I'm eighteen."

"Eighteen," Kennington repeated. "I'll bet you're still growing chest hair." He fingered Paul's open collar.

"When you were my age, you were on your second European tour," Paul said, wriggling.

"I was very bad in those days. I was always threatening to hurt my hands."

"Hurt them?"

"You know, stick them into alligators' mouths."

"You're joking —"

"And once I put my right hand into the garbage disposal and threatened to turn it on. My mother had to switch off the circuit breakers."

"Why did you do that? Stop, you're tickling me."

"To scare people. You must be tired from your flight."

"Not tired enough that I wouldn't have hurried over to your concert if it had been tonight. I would have given anything to hear you play the Chopin B-flat minor sonata. And speaking of the B-flat minor sonata, I meant to ask you, do you take the first-movement repeat —"

"I know when I get off a long flight, there's nothing I like better than a nice backrub."

"And if you do —"

"Want me to give you one? Get up. That's right." He sat in Paul's chair. "Now sit down. On the floor. Good." Hard legs enfolded Paul, who felt a sudden yanking on his shoulders.

He made a sound.

"Too deep?"

"No, it's okay. The fact is, I've never had a backrub. And you've got big hands. Me, I've got smallish hands. Ow! Miss Novotna says it doesn't matter, not everyone has hands like Rachmaninoff's."

He splayed his fingers. Kennington, taking his right hand from Paul's shoulder, pressed it against the open palm.

"Mine's not that much bigger."

"Are you kidding? Your forefinger must be half an inch longer than mine. But to get back to the B-flat minor —"

"Don't you ever talk about anything except music?"

"Sure . . . lots of things."

Curling his fingers inside Paul's, Kennington pulled them into a double fist. "Then let's make a deal," he whispered in Paul's ear. "Let's agree not to talk about music anymore, at least tonight."

"Fine." Paul stared at the conjoined entity of their hands.

Letting go, Kennington resumed his backrub. "So tell me something about yourself, Paul. After all, if we're going to be friends, it hardly seems fair that you should know so much about me when I don't know anything about you."

"What do you want me to tell you?"

"Whatever you feel like."

"Well, let's see . . . I was born on February 29, so I only have a birthday every four years. In Boston. My family's from Boston, originally. We moved west when I was eight."

"And what do your parents do for a living?"

"My father owns a printing business. My mother — she's a housewife, I guess, though she does volunteer work."

"Brothers and sisters?"

"One of each. They're older than me, and married."

"And are you married?"

"Of course not! I'm only eighteen."

"But you must have a girlfriend."

"No."

"A boyfriend?"

Paul said nothing.

"All right, now that I've interrogated you, you can ask me any questions you like, providing they're not musical."

"Well . . . I know you're not married. Do *you* have a girl-friend?"

"No."

"Oh."

"Why do you sound so surprised?"

"Well, I kind of assumed that you and Miss Strauss —"

"Tushi?" Kennington laughed. "Oh, I'm afraid I'm much too old for Tushi."

"But isn't she older than you?"

"Not enough for her taste."

Paul was quiet again. Closing his eyes, he started to relax into the rhythm of Kennington's hands.

"Good, you're loosening up. A long flight is hell on the

shoulders." Kennington stopped rubbing. "Say, I have an idea. Why don't you lie down on the bed? That way I can give you a proper massage."

Nodding, Paul stood.

"You can put your clothes on the chair," Kennington continued.

"My clothes!"

"I can't very well massage you through your clothes, can I?"

"I see your point," Paul agreed and, turning away, he began, somewhat cautiously, to unbutton his shirt. Kennington watched him. In truth, his own brazenness appalled him a little: after all, the proffered massage is easily the most cynical of seduction tactics, for isn't the essence of cynicism to cover lecherous intent with the thinnest veil of propriety, so thin that anyone who fails to see through it has only himself to blame? And yet he hardly believed Paul had come to his hotel room at nine in the evening just to talk about octaves.

Finally he finished with the shirt. "I'll just grab a towel," Kennington said, and went into the bathroom.

When he returned, towel and skin lotion in hand, Paul was standing by the chair in his underwear. In lieu of the usual briefs, he wore immense white boxer shorts, bloomers practically, at the sight of which Kennington couldn't help but laugh.

"What's so funny?"

"I'm sorry. It's just that those boxer shorts remind me of my father's."

"They're from Brooks Brothers," Paul said defensively.

"And anyway, what's wrong with them? They're comfortable. And if they're not like what boys my age usually wear, so what? I'm not like most boys my age. I've always preferred a more classic style of dress."

"Yes, of course. You're perfectly right. I apologize if I've embarrassed you."

"You haven't embarrassed me."

"You'd better take off your T-shirt too," Kennington added, opening the lotion bottle.

"I was just going to." Slowly he pulled the T-shirt over his head, where it caught on his glasses. He wrestled with it. A spray of fine pimples, Kennington noticed, fanned out over his pale shoulder blades.

"So where do you want me to lie down?" he asked, once he'd gotten out of the T-shirt.

"Here." Kennington spread the towel out on the bed.

Paul took off his glasses. "This is a comfortable mattress."

"Do you think so? You're welcome to sleep on it any time you want."

"Oh, but I've got my own room! Of course it's not as nice as this one. And smaller. Still, I like it. There's this window that . . . ow, that lotion's cold!"

"It'll warm up in a second." Under Kennington's hands, Paul's body gave off a faint, sweet staleness.

"You know what Miss Novotna once told me? She told me that Cecile Barrière — she was one of her pupils — has it written into her contracts to have a massage at every hotel she stays in."

"Sounds like Cecile."

"Is she a friend of yours?"

"An acquaintance."

"Then maybe you can tell me what the thing is with her Haydn disc. I know it got a great review in *Gramophone*. Even so —"

Kennington slapped lightly at the back of Paul's head. "I thought we'd agreed not to talk about music."

"I forgot."

"Why don't you shut up and just relax? You're never going to play Chopin until you learn to relax."

"Okay."

"Good." Kennington breathed. He touched the backs of Paul's calves very lightly, so that goosebumps rose.

Outside the rain started up again, a steady drumming against the window.

"Relax," Kennington incanted. "That's right." Bending over, he kissed Paul's neck.

Instantly Paul tensed.

"Hey, you're shivering," Kennington said. "You'd better get under the covers."

"I'm sorry. I'm afraid you've misunderstood — or maybe I have."

"Misunderstood what?"

"Why I came here."

"Why did you come here?" Kennington pursued.

"To see you. Not because . . . I mean, how can you know what you're like if you haven't done anything?"

"You can't," Kennington said. And switching the lights off, he began, in the dark, to unbuckle his watch.

"Are you all right?"

"Fine."

"But you didn't —"

"It doesn't matter."

Climbing out of the bed, Paul started pulling on his boxer shorts.

"Don't you want to take a shower?" Kennington asked, turning on the light for him.

"It's okay, I don't need to. Say, I really had a great time tonight. And thank you for the —"

"Paul, slow down."

He stopped, turned and gazed frankly at Kennington, who got out of bed, walked toward him, put his hands on his shoulders. "There's no need to rush," he whispered.

"But I'm tired. More tired than I've ever been in my life."

"Then why don't you sleep?"

"Because I have to get back. My mother will be worried."

"Are you sharing a room?"

"No."

"Then how will she know?"

"You haven't met my mother. Knowing her, she probably went down to the lobby and checked to see if the key was in the box."

Pulling away, Paul reached for his trousers, turned his T-shirt right side out. Kennington sat down on the bed. A sparse line of hairs, like sentries, marched from Paul's navel into his pants. Then the hairs disappeared inside the T-shirt, the T-shirt inside the shirt. Socks and shoes went on last. It was like watching a film run backward.

Finally he pulled on his jacket, patted his pants pocket, his breast pocket, his wrist.

"Wallet, watch, keys," he said. "Only tonight I don't have keys." He held out his hand. "So, good night. Thank you."

"Paul —"

"I'll never forget this evening . . . obviously."

"Let me ask one thing. Did I make a mistake tonight? Did I lead you into something you weren't ready for?"

"No, of course not."

"Because I assumed that when you came here, well, that this was what you came here for."

"I'm not sure why I came here," Paul said. "A lot has happened. It's been a long day and I'm tired."

"I understand."

"So, good-bye."

"Good-bye." They shook. Kennington walked him to the door, where Paul turned.

"You do realize," he said, "that I love you."

Kennington opened his mouth.

Paul left.

Kennington sat down. All day he'd been in an ill humor, only some of the reasons for which need be enumerated here: loneliness, the approach of forty, a nasty article in *The Boston Globe* that accused him of "perverting" Schubert. It had been his intention tonight to assuage that ill humor with bourbon and the writing of letters he would not end up sending; then, when Paul arrived, to assuage it with the sort of sexual despoiling that elegant hotel rooms always seemed to adore. Yet was it possible that Paul had come simply to — no, not to talk about music; that was *too* simple; perhaps, then, to look for something even the name of which he didn't know? In which case the shock of simultaneously learning what he wanted and getting it — it might have been too much.

The phone rang. Hoping it might be Paul, Kennington hurried to answer.

"Hello?"

"I've been trying to reach you all night. Were you at dinner?"

"Just taking a walk."

"Oh, that sounds nice. Walking through the streets of old Rome." Across an ocean, Joseph Mansourian sucked on his cigarette. "So listen, I'm afraid I have some bad news. Sophie's not doing too well."

"Really? What's wrong?"

"Well, yesterday Maria called me at work and said she was having trouble breathing, so in the afternoon I took her over to Dr. Wincote, who thinks it's time . . . you know, to put her to sleep. And I understand his point. Still, I just can't. Not while she keeps looking up at me that way."

"I'm sorry, Joseph."

"And it's not like she's in pain or anything. She's eating. Most of the day she just lies on the kitchen floor, and she seems peaceful." Another drag on the cigarette. "So for the moment, I've decided to wait. Do you think it's the right decision?"

"I suppose, as long as she's not in pain."

"That's my feeling, too. And I'm glad you agree because it's tough having to ignore Dr. Wincote's advice, him being the professional." He coughed. "Well, and how are you doing over there?"

"Fine. Relaxing."

"By the way, I got an e-mail from the Santa Cecilia people. They were thrilled with the concert. They want you back next year."

"Wonderful."

"Oh, and speaking of Santa Cecilia, I hope you're not planning to skip that dinner tomorrow night with Mr. Batisti."

"What do you mean, skip it?"

"Just . . . well, Richard, you know as well as I do, that in the past, you've sometimes forgotten —"

"Forgotten is not the same as skipped. Say what you mean. You want to make sure I don't stand Batisti up."

"No!" Another inhalation. "Look, let me start again. I only want to stress, as your manager, the importance of this dinner in terms of your career. After all, that's my job."

"I know it's an important dinner."

"Okay, so long as that's clear. Anyway, not much other news from here, except — oh yes, I had dinner with Tushi last night. She has a new young man. A doctor."

"Handsome?"

"And twenty-seven."

"May we all be so fortunate as Tushi."

"Yes, she does look fantastic, considering her age. What?" A hand muffled the phone. "Listen, I'd better run. Accounting's been keeping an eye on my phone bills, if you can believe it. Last week they actually sent me a pissy memo suggesting that I should try to go easier on the overseas calls. Me, they send this memo to! As if there'd even be a company without me." Almost audibly, he shook his head. "And here I am, babbling on about how I'm not supposed to babble on."

Silence.

"Well, I'll let you go. You must be tired. When are you flying back?"

"Saturday, I think. I'm still not sure."

"It doesn't matter as long as you're back by the fourteenth." A pause. "You will be back by the fourteenth, won't you?"

"Of course. What do you take me for?"

"I just wanted to make sure. . . . Well, sweet dreams. I miss you."

"I miss you, too."

Another pause. "I love you."

"I love you, too."

"Good night, darling."

"Good night."

Kennington hung up. Over the course of the conversation something white near the curtain had caught his eye. Now, putting down the receiver, he went to see what it was. A piece of paper, folded in eighths, shone bright against the carpet.

Unfolding it, he read, "Summit Printing, Inc." Then:

Dear Paul,

   I have left your mother. I am in love with Muriel Peete
from the office. We plan to marry as soon as we obtain our
divorces. I'm sorry if this news comes as a shock, but I am
53 yrs. old and cannot continue living a lie . . .

After he finished the letter, he refolded it and put it in the
breast pocket of his jacket. Then he pulled open the curtain
and looked out onto the street. It was empty except for a boy
walking two poodles. What the Germans call an ear worm
had tunneled into his head, as always, some insidious ditty
from his childhood. "Good morning, good morning, We've
slept the whole night through . . ."

*And the whole night,* he thought, *it will play in my dreams . . .
if I sleep at all.*

He let the curtain fall shut. The boy with the poodles
turned the corner. On the glass, against which the rain slanted
ceaselessly, the glare of a streetlamp illuminated five oily
moons where his fingers had rested.

# 5

SOPHIE DIED that afternoon. This wasn't really such a tragedy, Joseph tried to convince himself. After all, she'd had a good life, had lived to be thirteen — old for a dachshund. Still, as he hailed a cab outside Dr. Wincote's office, a sensation of hollowness rose up in his stomach. His breathing got choppy. Safe inside the taxi, he had to loosen his tie. "Central Park West and Sixty-third," he told the driver, who made an efficient U-turn, scissoring his way through the clotted midday traffic. He was an older fellow — that is, older than Joseph — and his name was Manny Litwak. "Pretty rare you get a cabbie these days who speaks English," Joseph said.

"Most of the guys out there, they're immigrants," the cabbie answered. "Puerto Ricans, Russians."

"Yeah, the other day, I had an Oriental? I said to him, 'I need to go to White Street.' 'What street?' he kept asking me. 'White Street.' 'What street?' I tell you, it was like an Abbott and Costello routine."

They turned onto Broadway.

"White Street's down in Tribeca," Joseph added. "I've got a friend who has a loft there."

"I know where White Street is."

"Of course. I didn't mean to sound insulting. I'm not myself today because my dog just died. I'm on my way back from the vet's."

"Sorry to hear it."

"Thanks. It's strange, coming back empty-handed. And when I think that just an hour ago, I was riding downtown, her in my arms. My Sophie. She was thirteen."

"Pretty old for a dog."

"And then I had to pay the bill. Isn't it strange that even when something dies, you still have to pay the bill?"

The driver did not respond. Leaning back, Joseph found himself remembering the afternoon he and Kennington had driven out to the house of the breeder lady in Morristown, watched as she extracted Sophie from the wriggling mass of the litter: "like a furry worm," Kennington said later. That same week, he had moved into the loft on White Street, and Sophie had peed on the antique Bokhara, leaving a dark stain.

On Central Park West, the traffic eased. Because the driver knew the exact speed at which to coast in order to make all the green lights, they arrived at Joseph's building in a matter of minutes. Climbing out, he tipped too lavishly — payola for his need to confide — then stumbled toward the revolving door, where Hector, the handsomest of the doormen, awaited him.

"Afternoon, Mr. Mansourian," Hector said. "Everything go okay?"

"I'm afraid not, Hector. I'm afraid Sophie's passed on."

Hector's brow tensed, but it was the fabric braids glinting on his wide shoulders that captured Joseph's attention.

"Gosh, Mr. Mansourian, I'm sorry to hear that. She was a nice dog."

"Thank you."

"I know what it's like. A couple of years ago my mother lost her dog. Tidbit, we called him, on account of he was so small. It was very upsetting."

"Yes, it always is. You love them like children, you know?"

"I know, sir." With which regretful observation Hector pushed the revolving door. When he'd first moved into the building, twenty-five years ago now, it had amazed Joseph that people could be paid just to push revolving doors. Of course he hadn't understood then about unions. (Now he understood all too well about unions.) A certain grasping cynicism underlay the mechanics of New York luxury, he reflected, as the smooth and oiled gyre took him in, its brushed undersides scraping softly against the polished marble, ushering him through a multiplicity of reflections — like Alice through the looking glass, he sometimes thought. Then he was in the lobby. Ghosts of perfumes collided amid the dark wood veneers, the hard little pink sateen sofas and chairs that no one ever used — indeed, that seemed designed to repel use. And how many times had he passed through this lobby with Sophie, or with Kennington and Sophie, on the way back from the park? . . . but he didn't want to conjure Kennington right now. Funny that because Sophie had died,

Joseph should find himself grieving Kennington's absence, when he was merely in Europe, as he'd been dozens of times before; would be coming back soon, very soon, in time for their anniversary. Twenty years, they told people, not mentioning, for the sake of discretion, the first five, during which Kennington had been underage. Meanwhile a second doorman, this one elderly, was ringing for the elevator, which was an old-fashioned one, with a little velvet bench on which Joseph had never once seen anyone sit.

"Afternoon, Sam," Joseph said.

"Afternoon, Mr. Mansourian."

"I'm afraid my dog has passed on, Sam."

"Has he, now?"

"She. Sophie was a she."

"A real crying shame," Sam said — a little mockingly, Joseph thought — and he opened the doors for Joseph to step through.

Silently the doors closed on Joseph's face.

Almost as soon as the elevator started moving, he felt faint again, so much so that for the first time in twenty-five years, he actually sat down on the little velvet bench. This turned out to be more trouble than it was worth, as the ride took all of forty seconds. Up onto his feet he hoisted himself, before continuing into the cramped corridor, where he undid the double doors with their triple locks. In the front hall a black-and-white checkerboard of tiles stretched to the shadowed living room. He smelled cooking, heard Mozart — both from other apartments.

Once safe in his bedroom, he changed out of his suit; checked his e-mail (there was none), checked his voice mail (there was none). And what next? He wasn't sure. A planless evening stretched ahead of him. Of course he knew better than to go into the kitchen, where on the other side of the swinging door Sophie's bright red dishes still sat, one half filled with kibble and the other with water in which little bits of kibble floated, bloated, disintegrated. Her toys lay idle in the dog bed. He'd noticed the blood when he'd picked her up to take her to Dr. Wincote. And then, in the taxi on the way downtown, she had died without drama. No, he decided, in the end it was better to steer clear of the kitchen tonight; better, in the morning, to let Maria remove "the effects" with that harrowing efficiency that was her hallmark, so that when Joseph returned from the office the next afternoon the apartment would be scraped clean of all signs of canine life; except from photographs, no one would be able to tell that for years a dachshund named Sophie had lived here.

Still shaking a little, he went into the living room, where he mixed himself a drink and put on a CD: the adagietto from Mahler's Fifth Symphony. Then he sat down. He was wondering whether he should tell Kennington about Sophie. It was one-thirty in the morning in Rome, which meant Kennington would either be asleep, or out walking, or out at the bars; if he went to the bars, that is; if he did anything along those lines. And anyway, did the expected death of an old, sick dog really constitute enough of an emergency to justify a phone call in the middle of the night? Probably not. Probably better to call Tushi, who was in town. Or his mother in Queens. Except that Tushi was a cat person; his mother was dead. Ridiculous, that even after so much time passed, he should still want to call her. Another sign that he was becoming senile. Floating, bloating.

Or he could call someone else.

At the prospect, his fingers tingled.

From a side table, he picked up a magazine with a shirtless man on the cover; flipped through it; ran down the list of photographs and descriptions with his pencil, until he landed on one that he liked.

He reached for the phone and dialed.

To his surprise, a human voice answered.

"Good evening, this is Matt."

"Hello, Matt. I just saw your ad in *Advocate Classifieds*. I was wondering if you were free for an outcall."

"When?"

"Tonight, if possible."

"Give me your number and I'll call you back."

Joseph gave the number; hung up. Instantly the phone rang.

"Sorry about that. I've got to verify the calls. It's a matter of security."

"I understand."

"Anyway, my terms are two hundred for an hour, three hundred for two hours, five hundred for an overnight."

"An hour should be fine."

"I'm downtown. Where are you?"

"Upper West Side." Joseph gave the address.

"I should be able to get there in about twenty minutes. Oh, and you have to cover my cab fare."

"Of course."

"My name's not really Matt, by the way. It's Kenneth."

"Kenneth, I'm Joseph."

"Good, Joseph. Well, see you soon."

"Sounds good."

They hung up. Immediately Joseph switched off the adagietto. In his hall closet he kept a supply of cheap towels, which he now spread over the bed. Then he took a shower and dried himself before the mirror. And what did he see? A man who, at sixty-one, might have been an advertisement for the force of gravity, which pulls everything down, down. "Face or figure," he remembered his mother saying. "Every woman makes the choice." Only in his case it hadn't been a choice. Face had chosen him. In his clothes, he was a handsome man.

He put on his bathrobe, mixed himself another drink, then made his final preparations for the rendezvous, which consisted of putting his credit cards and passport in the safe, along with whatever small, tempting valuables happened to catch his eye. As an afterthought he slipped off his watch and put that in the safe as well. Finally he settled down in the living room and turned on the television. To his horror a dog food commercial filled the screen; he flipped past it quickly. On a Japanese soap opera, two women knelt on tatami mats and spoke earnestly. He could not understand a word they were saying.

After a while the buzzer rang. "A Mr. Kenneth to see you," he heard Hector call through the intercom.

"Send him up," Joseph answered, and went to wait by the front door. Above the elevator a familiar sprite of light climbed through the numbers, until the doors opened, and a tall, slightly weather-beaten young man in sweatpants and a leather jacket stepped out. "Hi," he said, holding out a thick hand. "I'm Kenneth."

"Kenneth, Joseph."

Joseph shut the door behind them. "This is a nice apartment," Kenneth said, taking off his jacket.

"I'm glad you think so. Would you like a drink?"

"A beer, if you've got one." Sitting on the sofa, he started untying his tennis shoes.

"One beer coming up," Joseph said, and almost automatically went into the kitchen. He was there before he knew it, confronting the twin red bowls from which, as he opened the refrigerator, he tried (and failed) to avert his eyes. Just as quickly he had fetched the beer and carried it back to Kenneth, who was struggling with a knot in one of his shoelaces. Finally he got it undone; kicked off the shoe.

Handing Kenneth the beer, Joseph sat opposite him, on the sofa.

"So where are you from, Kenneth?"

"Kansas City."

"Been in New York long?"

"About fifteen years."

"Ah." Joseph's upper lip twitched as he watched Kenneth pop the beer. "I'm from New York myself. Queens, actually."

"I don't know about you," Kenneth said, gulping from his beer, "but I'm kind of hot. Mind if I take off my shirt?"

"Feel free."

He yanked the T-shirt over his head. His chest was shaved, stubbly, tanned to a synthetic coffee color. "Very nice," Joseph said, as standing, he moved to run his fingers over the warm skin.

Kenneth stepped slightly back. "Mind if we take care of the money first?"

"Oh, of course not. Excuse me." Removing his hands, Joseph backed away, to the bureau, from the drawer of which he extracted his wallet.

Kenneth was undoing the drawstring of his sweatpants.

"So you said two hundred for an hour, is that right?"

"Yup. Plus twelve for the taxi."

Joseph counted out bills. "The fact is, I've never been to Kansas City, though I've been just about everywhere else in this godforsaken land. Let's see, twenty, forty, sixty, eighty." Suddenly he stopped. "Oh, dear. Oh, I can't believe this. This never happens. Let me —" Again he counted.

Then he smiled across the room. "This is very embarrassing," he said, "and I don't know quite how it happened, but I don't seem to have enough cash on hand. I have — let me

count it again — eighty-four dollars. But that's not possible! I
got money this morning! Oh, the vet, of course. I had to pay
the vet in cash. You see, my dog died today." He sat down.

Kenneth said nothing. Already he had his shirt back on,
was tying up his shoes.

"I'm sorry," Joseph went on. "You wouldn't by any chance
take a check, would you? Or a credit card?"

"I turned down another job for this."

"I really do apologize. I'm not in the habit of doing this sort
of thing."

Kenneth was dressed again. Joseph saw him to the door.

"Let me at least give you forty dollars for your trouble,"
he said.

"I turned down another job for this," Kenneth repeated.

"Then eighty." He handed Kenneth the bills. "Sorry
again."

Kenneth said nothing. Folding the money in his fist, he
stepped through the door, which Joseph closed and latched
without a word. Sitting down on the floor, Joseph listened for
the elevator. For some reason he was remembering a summer
afternoon not so many years ago when, driving toward Rome,
he and Kennington had had to stop for cows crossing the
road. The sound of the bells they wore around their necks was
almost music, almost an echo of cows' voices.

Amazing, memory's trick of seeming random, when of
course there is always a key: in this case, Italy. Rome. Where
Kennington, for all Joseph knew, might be sleeping; might
be fucking; might be dead, or drunk, or stumbling down

streets the stones of which the torchlight had burned to a primeval intensity.

Only minutes ago, a boy . . . he winced. He hated sounding, or feeling, like Kennington's mother. Yet it was true: they'd gone to choose Sophie from the litter, and Kennington, just like a little boy, had fallen to the floor and let the puppies crawl all over him. They'd licked his face, licked, when he laughed, the bright polished surfaces of his teeth, while Joseph watched, and the breeder lady smiled. "I can see your son's a real dog lover," she'd said.

"Yes," he'd echoed. "You're a real dog lover, aren't you, son?" Somehow calling him "son," as he sometimes did in bed, excited him. But Kennington, in a heap of dachshunds, was too convulsed with laughter to answer.

# 6

"ENOUGH BLUE in the sky to make a Dutch boy a pair of pants," Pamela said. "Remember that?"

Paul, stirring sugar into his coffee, shook his head.

"Just an old expression your grandmother used to use. When we were going on a picnic, and it started to rain, she'd peek out the window, and say, 'We'll go if you can find enough blue in the sky to make a Dutch boy a pair of pants.' Well, what do you think, Pauly? Is there?"

He looked at the sky, where threads of clouds still drifted. He looked at his mother. She had on dark glasses. Nonetheless her features — yesterday discomposed by shock and uprooting — were starting to reassemble themselves. Yes, she was ceasing to be the walking disaster to whom pride alone lent some semblance of dignity, and becoming again the laughing woman she had usually been, the laughing woman Paul had always thought of her as being.

"I'd say yes," Paul said. It was eight in the morning, and they were breakfasting on the loggia of their hotel.

"Still, we ought to take umbrellas as a precaution. Oh, I'm so excited. I want to see the Colosseum, the Parthenon —"

"The Pantheon."

"The Pantheon, the Forum. Unless of course you'd rather be by yourself. If that's the case, Paul, just tell me. I understand."

"No, no, we can sightsee together."

They got up. An inward sense of victory had turned the corners of Pamela's lips upward in the slightest smile. Something had happened. She didn't know why, but this morning, as she was finishing her make-up, Paul had barreled into her room and flung himself against her. "Sweetheart," she'd said, her arms going round him. "Honey, what's the matter?" But he hadn't answered.

People rarely admit it, Pamela observed to herself, but the sorrow of a beloved can be gladdening. Usually when he was upset, Paul pulled away from his mother, as he had last night. She'd had to train herself not to plead for his company. And then, when she least expected it, these hiccups of childhood would seize him, and something would freshen in her, especially as she knew they would come less and less frequently as the years passed, then not at all.

In the Pantheon, he read aloud to her from Georgina Masson. Beneath the enormous aperture at the center of the dome the marble, inset with little drains, was still wet from last night's storm. "Listen to this," he said. "In the niches there used to be statues of all the gods and goddesses, and according to Pliny, the statue of Venus wore as earrings two halves of a pearl Mark Anthony took from Cleopatra. And the pearl had a twin that she dissolved in vinegar and drank to win a bet."

"Cleopatra drank a pearl?"

Paul nodded.

"Ugh," Pamela said. "No thank you. Not for all the tea in China." Then they were pushed away by a bargelike woman who was leading a German tour group to Raphael's tomb with a flyswatter. "Until the twentieth century this was the largest dome in the world. Some of the bricks date from 125 A.D. And the interior — it says here, 'The concrete was mixed with travertine, tufa, brick and pumice stone in successive layers, with the heaviest materials at the lower levels, the lighter tufa and pumice mixture being used at the top of the dome.'" Paul shut his book. "It must have really been something before all this Christianizing."

"Must have been," his mother echoed.

They went out the immense bronze doors. Tiny cars, the smallest she had ever seen, buzzed around the piazza. Their wheels were half the size of those on her station wagon, and a few had only three of them.

"Look at that. That car doesn't even have a steering wheel, it has handlebars, like a motorcycle. And it's called an Ape."

"No, it's pronounced *ah-pay*. That means 'bee.'"

"So ape is bee and cold is hot. What a funny language." She pulled her scarf tighter around her neck. In fact she was more at ease talking about cars than the Colosseum, the dust of which smudged her shoes, and which in any event stank of urine. For the architecture of Rome was not only monumental, it was monumentally indifferent. It bore down. Thousands have come and gone here, it seemed to say. Goethe, Liszt. You do not matter.

They went into more churches than she could keep track of. In one of them Paul started reading to her about the apse. She was too embarrassed to admit that at forty-seven years old she didn't know what an apse was. And then all the ruins started to seem to her to be just so much stone and earth. Unlike Paul, she couldn't extrapolate a temple from two columns of marble. Rome to her was dirt, deadness.

When they finished their touring they took a walk down the Via Condotti. In the shops saleswomen in ruthlessly tailored little suits followed them everywhere, as if they were thieves. These women's shoes were not scuffed. There wasn't a wrinkle on them. Whereas Pamela, in her black slacks and wrinkled blouse, might as well have had a sign taped to her back that read "TOURIST." Every shopkeeper addressed her automatically in English. No wonder the little gypsy girls in their filthy patterned skirts and shawls flocked to her in front of the Spanish Steps! When it happened, Paul was across the piazza, buying a newspaper. Suddenly a bevy, several pregnant, had surrounded Pamela. They thrust torn maps and dirty pieces of cardboard into her abdomen. At first she thought they were asking directions. "I don't speak Italian!" she told them, as quick hands slipped inside her purse. It was all rather dreamy. "Stop that!" she said, slapping them away. "Stop it! Paul!"

He turned. "I'm coming!" he called. Then a tall man intervened, whacking at the girls with his umbrella. "*Andate via!*" he shouted, grabbing one by her ponytail. The girl howled, while her friends laughed, flurried, regathered like skittish birds a few feet off.

"*Dai,*" the tall man said to the girl, who was trying to pull away from him.

She spat.

"*Dai,*" he repeated, his voice grim, yanking at her ponytail to hurt her.

She thrashed. The other girls lingered on the periphery and shouted for him to leave her alone.

"*Va be', va be'!*" the girl said finally, a bright red wallet dropping from her skirt.

The tall man pushed her away, picked up the wallet, handed it to Pamela.

"Everything in order?"

"I think so."

Rubbing the back of her head where he had hurt her, the girl hissed imprecations at him. In her strange language she vowed that he would suffer headache his whole life, that his first-born child would die, that he would lose every good thing he had.

Then some *carabinieri* rode into the piazza on their horses. She hurried off.

"Thank you so much." In unconscious sympathy with her attacker, Pamela touched the back of her head. "I can't tell you how grateful —" She stopped speaking. "But you're —"

Across the fountain, Paul watched, his eyes narrow.

"Have we met before?" Kennington asked. He asked the question of Pamela, but he was looking at Paul.

It really was a coincidence. That morning Kennington had just been coming out of the Caffè Greco, when he'd noticed Paul and his mother gazing into a shop window on the Via Condotti. Paul was wearing a neatly pressed white shirt and khaki trousers. His mother, who had a large quantity of dark blond hair, came up only to his shoulder.

His first impulse was to run up and greet them. Then he thought better of it and, hurrying back into the caffè, watched them through the door. In front of the shop they were laughing . . . at what? The designs? The prices? Or was it that nervous laughter, as he knew from experience, people so often emit upon being told something they think ugly is actually beautiful?

Finally Paul's mother linked her arm through his, and they continued down the street.

Like a spy, Kennington followed them.

In the Piazza di Spagna, Paul went to a kiosk and bought a newspaper. It was then that the gypsy girls attacked his mother. Speaking to her had never been Kennington's intention; indeed, his intention had been simply to watch; to try to gauge, from the way they interacted, how much Paul might have told her. But then the mother was in trouble, and he had no choice but to intervene, his own mother having brought him up to be chivalrous to ladies. Pamela looked dazed, so he took them back to the Caffè Greco, where under a framed photograph of Buffalo Bill (he had customed there in 1903) they drank coffees, hers with a little grappa added. "I really can't thank you enough, Mr. Kennington," she said. "It all happened so quickly. One minute I was just standing there admiring the steps and the next those little fingers were everywhere. I mean, I assumed they were only asking directions!"

"Never underestimate gypsy children," Kennington answered. "Their parents train them by making them stick their hands in bowls of broken glass. You have to be just as quick, and just as brutal."

"Well, you're certainly my hero today." She brushed hair out of her eyes. "You know, it's only our first morning here? That wallet had everything in it. Credit cards, traveler's checks. We're alone here in Rome, you see. My husband and I are separated."

"Ah."

"And what a coincidence! At breakfast Paul was telling me that he saw the poster for your concert."

Kennington looked at Paul, who was studying the foamy residue at the bottom of his cup.

"Also, your Italian is so good! Where did you learn it?"

"Here and there. I had an Italian teacher for a while."

"Aldo Minchilli, right?" Paul interposed.

"Right."

"Well, Mr. Kennington, you simply must let us take you to lunch. To thank you."

"On the contrary, you must let me take *you* to lunch."

"But that's ridiculous —"

"I insist."

"But there's no reason —"

"Exactly."

As with the barman, the force of masculine will proved indomitable. "Okay," Pamela said. "How about we just go to lunch and then decide who pays? Does that sound all right?"

They went. The owner of the trattoria to which Kennington led them called him maestro and kissed Pamela on the hand. "And how is Mr. Mansourian?" he wanted to know.

"Fine, fine," Kennington said, while through the archway that opened onto the kitchen, a young cook ran his fingers through a pile of freshly cut fettuccine as tenderly as if it were his lover's hair.

"This is so wonderful!" Pamela said when the first courses arrived. "And such a far cry from the stuff we're used to back home! You know, mushy spaghetti in watery sauce."

"It's a good place. I always try to come here when I'm in Rome."

"Do you come often? Are you on tour?"

"The poster Paul saw was for the last of my Italian concerts."

"What an exciting life you must lead, traveling all the time and staying in hotels."

Kennington smiled, not sure how to explain that like most people who spend most of their lives in hotels, they no longer held much glamour for him.

"The funny thing is, I've probably been to Rome a dozen times, and I've hardly done any sightseeing. It's always been too hectic. You know, interviews, lunch, interviews, concert, boring official dinner. Then the next morning you leave. Now I've decided to stay on a bit. Do you know I've never even been to the Sistine Chapel?"

"You should have Paul take you around. He's a wonderful tour guide, aren't you, honey? Today we did the Colosseum, the Parthenon —"

"The Pantheon."

"The Pantheon, all kinds of churches. Unfortunately we're only here a week or so. After that we go up to Florence."

"So you're a student of the classical world as well as the piano?" Kennington asked Paul.

"I read up before our trip, if that's what you mean."

"Sweetheart, you really should take Mr. Kennington around this afternoon. Show him the sights. Me, I've got to get my hair done. All day I've been looking at these chic Roman ladies and I feel like a frump. What do you say?"

"Don't you think you ought to ask if he *wants* to be taken around?"

"Actually, I'd love it."

Paul looked surprised, almost resentful.

"Wonderful, then it's settled. You two drop me off at the hairdresser, then go and see everything. And maybe we can meet later — that is, if you're free, Mr. Kennington."

"In fact," Kennington said, "I have nothing scheduled for the rest of my life."

Pamela laughed. "Oh, I doubt that —"

"Please call me Richard."

"Richard." She wiped her lips.

As at the concert, Paul would not meet Kennington's eye.

Even though it wasn't far, Kennington took them back to his hotel in a taxi. "I can't vouch for him," he said, "but I'm told the hairdresser here is very good."

"I'm sure. Oh, what a magnificent lobby! The place we're staying is very simple. Characteristic, though. They serve breakfast on the loggia."

"Tell me the name. I may move. I can't bear these stuffy places."

"Albergo Bernini —"

Approaching the concierge, Kennington said something in rapid Italian.

"Good, then everything's all set. The concierge will take you to Mr. Frank."

The concierge, who had a greased gray mustache, inclined his head. "Good-bye!" Pamela called as he led her away. "Thank you! Have fun."

"Bye."

"See you at seven in front of the Trevi Fountain!"

She disappeared around a trompe l'oeil bend.

Kennington turned to Paul. "I'm sorry about that," he said. "I never intended —"

"It's okay. I'm afraid my mother's a bit of a hysteric."

"The thing was — I wanted to give you this." And he handed Paul his father's letter.

"Oh."

"It must have dropped out of your pocket. I have to admit, I read it, to see what it was. And I just want to say, Paul, if I'd realized the pressure you were under —"

"Am I under pressure? I don't feel like I'm under pressure."

"But taking care of your mother —"

"Oh, I've always taken care of my mother. I'm used to that."

"Well, in any case, if I'd realized, I certainly wouldn't have been quite so aggressive. About the sex, I mean. That isn't my style. Usually I take pride in a certain . . . gentlemanly demeanor."

"You really don't need to explain," Paul said, folding up the letter.

"But I do. I lost control of myself, I . . . there's no other way to say it, I let lust get the better of me. For which I'm sorry."

Paul hardly knew how to respond. Nothing in his education had prepared him for such a conversation.

"Apology accepted," he said finally — what else could he say? — "but not necessary."

"Thanks." They were silent for a moment. "Anyway, I'm glad I found you again."

"So am I."

"You are?"

"Of course. You can't be surprised."

"No, I . . . actually, I am a bit. Surprised and happy." Like a child, he clapped his hands, then threw an arm around Paul's shoulder. "And what would you like to do this afternoon? We could climb up to the Campidoglio, or look at churches, or" — he hesitated — "we could go up to my room . . ."

Paul shrugged.

They went up to the room.

Just after seven they emerged again. "We're late," Paul said, looking at his watch. "My mother will be worried."

"Relax," Kennington said. "We can take a taxi."

But traffic turned out to be terrible, and they had to abandon the taxi on Piazza Barberini. Kennington's heels tapped loudly against the pavement as he fought the crowds surging down Via Nazionale. He was wearing chinos, a striped shirt, a blue blazer. Whereas Paul still had on the same clothes he'd put on that morning, albeit without underwear, his boxer shorts having remained behind in Kennington's bathroom.

"Let's go this way," Kennington said, and led Paul up a small side street, then into an empty alley, where he kissed him.

"I love you," Paul said for the second time. "Don't worry, you don't have to answer." He sucked the peppermint taste off Kennington's tongue.

"I guess we'd better go," Kennington said eventually.

"Wait. I can't go yet."

"Why not?"

"Just wait."

They waited.

"All right."

They moved on. In the piazza, couples were taking pictures of each other tossing coins over their shoulders into the fountain. Its aquamarine shallows glinted with currency. As for Pamela, she was standing alone at the rail, her arms gripped tightly around her waist, her eyes searching the crowd.

"Mom! Over here!"

She turned and waved. "Hello! Hello! Well, what do you know? I toss a coin into the fountain and wish for two handsome gentlemen to escort me to dinner. And now my wish comes true!"

"I'm sorry we're late," Kennington said. "We just got so caught up in seeing things —"

"Oh, don't worry, I've been fine! Just watching the world go by."

She threw back her new hair, which was cut short, blonder than it had been earlier, molded to bookend her face.

"Gorgeous," Kennington said.

"You like it? I have you to thank for it. And did Paul treat you okay?"

"Paul," Kennington said, "was stunning."

"He's so knowledgeable!" Pamela caressed his cheek. "As for me, I had an absolute ball. After my hair I got a manicure *and* a pedicure. Then I bought this new outfit. At Armani! Cost an arm and a leg, but that's what credit cards are for, right, Pauly?"

"Right," Paul said, as taking a hundred-lire coin from his pocket, he hurled it gamely into the fountain.

Across the city, meanwhile, in an elegant, otherwise empty restaurant in Parioli, Signore Giovanni Batisti of the Amici della Musica di Roma, his wife, and several prominent local citizens were sitting at a large table, drinking mineral water and eating stale bread.

"It's unusual for Americans to be so late," Signore Batisti said, looking at his watch as the clock struck the half hour.

"The poor man's probably stuck in traffic," his wife answered.

"Traffic! It's the construction on Via Arenula," said another man.

"And the smog!"

Signore Batisti shook his head. "Altogether I fear Rome may be making a very bad impression on Mr. Kennington."

A general murmur of concurrence.

And the waiter brought another bottle of mineral water.

# 7

THE BOYS were late again. At her table outside the Bar della Pace, Pamela checked her watch, nibbled a peanut, took a tiny sip from her mineral water. One of the mysteries of travel is that it telescopes ritual; thus, after only a few days, the three of them were already making it their habit to meet "every" afternoon at the Bar della Pace, and "every" afternoon the boys were late. She didn't mind — indeed, it was her intention to encourage the happy rapport that seemed to be blossoming between them — and yet if they could have been on time just once . . . well, she had to admit, it would have pleased her. (Not wishing them to find her with an empty glass, she drank another millimeter's worth of water.) For mightn't his efforts to win Paul over be part of a larger strategy? And if they were, what might that strategy be? If only he'd give her a clear signal . . . (She blushed at the thought of it, the hope of it, which kept her buoyed in the wake of Kelso's betrayal.) Meanwhile a cat leapt down from a parked car to beg for a peanut. Ivy, as well as shadows of ivy, climbed the stone walls. A Vespa pulled up to the bar, and a man in a black double-breasted suit climbed off of it, his thick graying hair closely cropped, his mustache plump. Smiling, he took the table next to hers. The cat ran off. He ordered a coffee, removed from his jacket pockets a cellular telephone, a lighter, and a pack of cigarettes, which he arranged carefully on the tabletop like attributes in a Bronzino portrait. From another pocket he extracted and put on a pair of sunglasses. "*Vuole?*" he asked, waving a cigarette in Pamela's direction.

"Oh, no thanks," she said. "*Grazie.* I don't smoke."

He smiled again, took off his sunglasses, stared at her face, her neck, her breasts. She was scandalized and thrilled. It occurred to her dimly that she was an attractive woman. In her marriage she had never thought of herself as an attractive woman. But now a Roman coin dangled from a thin gold chain between her breasts. She was wearing an ecru linen jacket and slacks from Armani, a white linen blouse with lace trim, Ferragamo shoes. All charged on Kelso's credit card.

Feeling bold, she smiled back. Then the boys arrived. They looked happy, sleepy. "Hello!" Pamela said, giving a backward glance to her admirer and trying to stifle — how odd! — a sense of disappointment.

"Pamela, you look magnificent."

"Thank you, Richard. Sit down, sit down. And tell me, what mischief did you two get up to today?"

"Well, first we went to the Baths of Caracalla," Paul said. (This was a lie. They had spent the entire day in Kennington's bed.)

"How wonderful. And was it everything you hoped?"

"Magnificent."

"After that we went to the archaeological museum, since we couldn't cover everything yesterday."

"That's why we were late."

"Oh, it doesn't matter your being late. As for me, I had a little adventure myself today." And she told a story about an old English lady she'd met at the Bernini. Like most of her stories, it became, in the telling, both longer and more discursive than the actual event that had inspired it. Kennington had trouble following the details, in part because her disheveled narrative technique discouraged linear comprehension, in part because under the table Paul was rubbing the toe of his shoe against Kennington's ankle. From the very labor of having to keep a straight face, he seemed to be deriving a perverse thrill.

After coffee, they did some more walking. It was turning out to be one of those gloriously bright Roman afternoons when the sunshine seems limitless. From a fruit seller's basket, scarlet peppers spilled out in obscene abundance. Two boys played soccer with an onion. A butcher's window displayed folded slabs of tripe and unplucked guinea hens, while next door, in a pasta shop, squat extrusion machines pumped out little tortellini like turds. *Italy,* Paul thought, *the country of which I am not,* while from a nearby bar (in Rome there is always a nearby bar) a waiter stepped out onto the street, bearing a tray on which rested three tiny cups of coffee, over each of which he had tucked a little paper napkin like a bonnet.

"Isn't that wonderful," Pamela said.

"Don't embarrass me by taking a picture," Paul said.

"Oh, Paul," Pamela said, and peered at some Murano glass candies in a window.

They had another coffee, standing up, at Caffè Greco ("our caffè," Pamela called it), then split up briefly, Pamela to exchange a blouse at Max Mara, Paul and Kennington to look at CDs at the Ricordi on Via del Corso. In the Piazza di Spagna, masses of tourists were aiming their cameras at the boat fountain. Few of them looked very happy, however, and when they conversed, their dialogue verged inevitably into indigestion, lost luggage, bad exchange rates.

Kennington was thinking that he had never much liked being a tourist. Tourism, in his view, was the apotheosis of an age of too much choice. Its anxiety was decision: where to stay, what to eat, whether to go by train or fly or rent a car. Which was ironic, when you considered that in the old Italy — the dust of which thousands of tourist feet unsettled daily — ordinary life offered a range of options so meager as to seem almost a parody of choice. In such a world, habit, not possibility, sustained human life.

He had often remarked to Joseph that probably he would have been happier living in that old peasant Europe, where amid slow harvests and patient cultivations, he could have worked away at his lot of years, eaten bread with olive oil, and died old: the very opposite of a public life, to which he considered himself temperamentally ill-suited. (In this respect he was the opposite of Joseph.) Music provided something of a solution, in that through music he gained a glimpse of eternity, a different scale of time. Yet music also meant photographers, and hotel rooms, and the *Gramophone* awards: the feedback of fame, Joseph called it; you could not hear your own voice for all the voices. You could not hear your own music for all the music. And so he dreamed of a homeplace to which he might retreat, maybe with a friend, and play for himself and his friend. *A private rapture of the keys* . . . Now other minds judged (and in these, his middle years, judged harshly).

Of course, he never actually fled to the homeplace. Vanity interfered — vanity, and terror. The furthest he ever got was failing to show up at dinners, and writing letters he never sent, and having affairs with young men he hoped would turn out to be "the friend," the most recent of these young men being Paul, who dreamed only of stages. And why not? Paul was eighteen, and ambitious, and craved *more* of the new: more adventure, more passion, more happiness, which he saw as a positive state, rather than merely the hiatus that comes when every item on a list has been checked off. Sometimes Kennington even sensed that it was all he could do to keep from throwing the affair in his mother's face. Love pushed him toward a boldness, even a recklessness, that only the speed bumps of his own anxiety kept in check.

"What do you think of my mother?" he asked now, as they strolled up Via del Babuino.

Kennington considered the question carefully. The truth was, he hadn't thought much of Paul's mother at all; to him, she was merely an obstacle, a source of trouble he needed to flatter in order to ensure that he and Paul could continue sleeping together. And yet to admit this might sound callous, since no matter how much Paul complained about her, she was still his mother.

He cleared his throat. "Pamela's a very nice woman," he said, adding as an afterthought, "clearly she adores you."

"She's always lived through me. A typical stage mother, really." They turned left, onto a side street. "Was your mother like that?"

"No, no. My mother was a very simple woman, very self-effacing. Oh, she encouraged me, took me to my lessons and came to my recitals and all that. And yet I always wondered whether she cared much, in the end. Then she deposited me into Joseph's hands, and he held the reins from there."

"And your father? You never talk about your father."

"My father was irrelevant," Kennington said simply. "He disappeared early. He doesn't signify."

Sidling past a truck that was taking up most of the street, Paul said, "Sometimes I wonder if my mother even has a clue as to what's going on between us."

"Better that she doesn't."

"But I get so tired of being careful! Of making up stories, and talking around things."

"It's important that you do, though. For her sake."

They had arrived at the Ricordi. Paul turned, looked at Kennington with disaffected curiosity. Then they went in.

In the classical department, he hurried to the piano section, where he dug out Kennington's first recording. "This was made in London, wasn't it?"

"Yes. Paul, please put that back. You're embarrassing me."

Paul waved the CD in Kennington's face, waved his own face in his face: younger, of course, and wearing glasses rather like the ones Paul wore now.

"What did it feel like, making it?"

"I was a kid. That afternoon Joseph had shown me how to shave."

"Had you ever been to Europe before?"

"I'd never been out of America before. Please put it back. Thank you."

"Was anyone else in your family musical?"

"They say my great-grandfather wrote 'Home on the Range,' but someone stole it from him. Hey, I thought —"

"Look, here's your encores disc! I love this record. What's the most encores you've ever played in concert?"

"Eight, I think."

"Where?"

"Was it Lyon? Lyon."

"What were they?"

"I'm not sure I remember —"

"Please?"

"Okay, let's see. The first, I think, was a Chopin waltz. And then I did Godowsky's transcription of 'The Swan.' That one was very moving for me because my teacher —"

"But that's not on the encores disc."

"True. As I was saying, Godowsky was important to me chiefly because —"

"By the way, I think this picture of you is the best anyone's taken."

"Probably."

"Whereas the best cover without a picture of you was on your Schubert record, without a doubt. Let's see if they have it —"

"I know what it looks like. Anyway, it's out of print."

"Oh, look at this. What do you think of four-hand repertoire?"

"It's fine."

"What do you think of repertoire for the left hand?"

"It's fine."

"I tried playing one of those Saint-Saëns études for the left hand once. What would you do if your right hand got mangled in some horrible accident? Would you start playing left-handed?"

"Probably I'd breathe a sigh of relief and retire forever. So do you want to buy anything?"

"All of *your* CDs I already have. How about you?"

Kennington shook his head. They left.

"I'm hyperventilating," he said on the street. "I'm not used to such youthful energy."

"You don't mean what you just said about retiring, do you?" Paul asked.

"Remember, I'm the man who stuck his hand into a garbage disposal. Like in *Carrie*."

"Why did you do it?"

"I was angry, and tired. I've never much liked public life, only playing. Playing — it's hard to explain."

"But playing *is* public."

"And there lies the dilemma of my life. I have the wrong personality for my talent."

"Better that than to have the wrong talent for your personality."

They turned a corner. Down Via dei Condotti Pamela waved colored bags at them.

"Remember what I told you," Kennington whispered. "Be careful."

"Oh, I will," Paul said, grabbing Kennington's arm and squeezing hard.

Before dinner, they made one last, and as Paul realized later, horribly ironic, touristic expedition: they went to see the Bocca della Verità, or Mouth of Truth, into which Pamela remembered watching Gregory Peck insert his hand in *Roman Holiday*. A fourth-century manhole cover, roughly carved into the shape of a human face, the Bocca now hung in the portico of the little church of Santa Maria in Cosmedin.

As usual, Paul read from his guidebook. "In the Middle Ages," he told Pamela and Kennington, "it was used for a sort of trial by ordeal to see if people — particularly wives suspected of unfaithfulness — were telling the truth. It was thought that if anyone told a lie while holding their right hand in the open mouth the terrible stone jaws would close, cutting off their fingers."

"How awful," Pamela said.

Paul shut his book. A string of couples, mostly Japanese, had formed a queue to the Bocca's left. One after another the wives put their right hands into the mouth; one after another the husbands took their pictures. Sometimes, in the click of the snapshot, the women would wince, as if they feared that what they were hearing was really the snap of jaws.

When there was a lull, Pamela asked Kennington to take her picture, which he did. "Now yours," she said.

"No, no," Kennington said. "I don't like being photographed."

"Oh, come on," Pamela pleaded. "Just one."

"Mom, when someone doesn't like being photographed —"

"But this isn't an album cover. It's just one little snapshot. Come on. Please?"

"Mom —"

"Okay, okay," Kennington said, and stepped over to the Bocca.

"Good," Pamela said. "Now stand there. Put your hand in, that's good. And be careful. Your fingers are more valuable than other people's."

"Hurry up, will you?"

"Hush, Paul, I just need to frame the picture . . . fine. Now tell a lie."

"A lie?"

"So we can see if the legend's true."

Kennington winced. "A lie . . . I just can't think of one. Okay, how about this? I love being a pianist. I love my life as a pianist."

The flash erupted. He winced.

"Oh, Richard. Playing it safe, are you? But who can blame you?"

Her face came into focus. He removed his hand.

# 8

"HOTEL BRISTOL."

"Maestro Kennington's room, please."

"I'm sorry, sir. He isn't back yet. Would you like to leave a message?"

"No, no. I've already left one. Just make sure it was slipped under his door. Joseph Mansourian."

"Yes, sir."

"He didn't happen to say when he'd be back, did he?"

"No sir."

"All right. Thank you. Good night."

"Good night."

Kennington, who really was in his room but had left instructions not to be disturbed, aimed the remote control at the television, flipping from station to station until he found CNN. Next to him, on the bed, Paul made paper airplanes.

"Tell me about Miss Novotna," he said.

"I'm not really the person to ask," Kennington said. "The truth is, I don't know her very well, given that she's supposedly responsible for my career."

"But how can that be? You must run into each other all the time at parties."

Kennington smiled. One of Paul's many naive notions was that adult life consisted chiefly of parties.

"My guess is that Olga's a very old-fashioned person, in a lot of fundamental ways. And I am too. So we made a sort of unspoken agreement to steer clear of each other after the Chopin, I suppose because the whole thing embarrassed us. It thrust us into an unnatural intimacy."

"What else can you tell me?"

"Well, you know she's from Texas, right?"

"I heard that."

"Novotna's the name some impresario gave her in the forties, I guess because he thought you had to have an Eastern European name to have a career. And then she did have something of a career, until she met Kessler." He looked across the bed at Paul. "You are aware that she was Kessler's lover, aren't you?"

"Of course. I've even asked her about it. She gave up her career for love of someone greater."

"As if she had any choice in the matter."

"What do you mean?"

"Kessler had a huge ego. He couldn't bear anyone horning in on his glory. The only people he allowed around him were either muses or toadies. You know two of his children killed themselves," Kennington added.

"No, I didn't."

"It's true. So Olga quit playing and became his mistress

full-time. Twenty, twenty-five years they were together. Mostly in Paris, though they traveled all the time. And during this whole period he never divorced his wife, and even went back to her periodically, all of which Olga put up with. Then when he died — you know he died quite suddenly — it turned out he hadn't made a single provision for her in his will. Everything went to the wife, who, as you can imagine, wasn't particularly inclined to make a little allowance for Olga." Kennington sighed. "After that it was too late for her to go back to playing. So she moved to San Francisco and started making her living teaching brats like you." He mussed Paul's hair.

"God," Paul said. "Where did you learn all of this?"

"Common knowledge." Kennington switched the television to the BBC. A long sheet of waxy paper was now worming its way under the door: a fax, no doubt from Joseph, who was nothing if not persistent. Already Kennington's bureau drawer was stuffed with faxes and little pink message slips, all of them urging him, he was sure, to call so that he could be chastised for having failed to show up at Signore Batisti's dinner.

Getting up off the bed, he picked up the fax and stuffed it, as well, into the bureau drawer.

"Aren't you going to read it?" Paul asked.

Kennington shook his head. "I'll read it later. What say we take a walk? It's beautiful out."

Reluctantly, Paul got up and put on his shoes. Out of the hotel they strode, up the Via Veneto and into the gardens of the Villa Borghese. "Mr. Mansourian must be a wonderful manager," Paul said.

"The best in the business."

"You must be very grateful. He's done a wonderful job by you."

"Has he? I thought I'd done the wonderful job."

"I didn't mean you hadn't. I only meant —" Paul grimaced. "Damn. I didn't . . ."

"It's okay." And he wondered, not for the first time, whether Paul's real purpose in this affair might not have been to obtain some sort of official introduction to Joseph. Kennington was famous, after all, and as Joseph was forever warning him, people always tried to take advantage of the famous, a cynical pronouncement against which, in the early days of their relationship, he had protested. Yet time and experience, instead of proving him wrong, had proved Joseph right, even about Joseph, whose own motives in souring a teenage boy against the advances of humankind could hardly be called altruistic. Above all else, he'd wanted to keep Kennington from leaving him.

They crossed a playground and entered into the forested region of the park. After nearly a week, Paul remained a muddle to Kennington. Even as he pestered, he intoxicated. Even as he annoyed, he beguiled. He could drink in sensation and pleasure with the gusto of a Pater, then suddenly lapse into a crabbed, almost clerical meticulousness. Nonetheless it was difficult for Kennington to resent his interruptions, which were frequent, or his insensitivities, which were slashing, because they reminded him so much of himself at the same age; also because he knew that these lapses derived not from inherent selfishness, or greed for attention, but rather from that extreme lassitude of self-knowledge for which he suspected his mother to be in no small part responsible. Though he was not an only child, his brother and sister were so much older than he was that he had ended up being raised in what amounted to a bubble of worship. It was into Paul alone that Pamela had sunk her store of hopes and ambitions: slipshod, hasty constructions, inclined to leakage or collapse, yet for all their shoddiness, as richly invested with pathos and intensity as, well, as the finest things Schubert ever built. For sadly, it is not only to the beautiful and the sound, Kennington knew, that people devote their souls.

Another word, now, about Kennington's own amorous career: because his work required him to travel in such a comparatively limited orbit, almost all the men with whom he'd had affairs over the years had been musicians. Not only did they know exactly who he was before they met him, they often admired, or loathed, him intensely. And the result was that he found himself, time and again, in bed with people who knew enormous amounts about him, yet about whom he knew absolutely nothing, a disturbing imbalance that often led him to question the veracity of their attraction. Were his invitations accepted because of what he looked like (itself, he admitted, a rather degraded criterion), or because of who he was? Even in Paul's case, he never felt quite certain. He had been tricked with sex before. The last time had been in New

York, the previous spring. Joseph was at the ASOL convention, which he liked to call the asshole convention, and Kennington was taking care of Sophie. One afternoon he was walking her in the park when a young man met his glance; followed him back to Central Park West; finally, after twenty minutes in a holding pattern, introduced himself, explaining that he rarely did this sort of thing, then plying Kennington with exactly the sort of erotic dialogue he could not resist; only later, when they had gone back to Joseph's apartment, and were kissing on the sofa, did the young man suddenly pull away. "I'm sorry," he said, sitting up. "I'm afraid there's something I haven't told you. I know who you are."

"Who I am?" Kennington repeated.

"Yes. You're Richard Kennington. I recognized you from the minute you started looking at me in the park. You see, I'm a piano student myself, at Mannes. And when I realized that *the* Richard Kennington was cruising me, I thought, how can I say no? The only problem is, I'm not physically attracted to you. I hope you don't mind. I like guys in their twenties." He grinned. "Maybe we could just talk instead?"

"Sure," Kennington answered, tucking in his shirt. After which they had gone together to a café, where he had been forced to endure exactly the sort of prolonged interview he most loathed, and at the end asked a favor. Needless to say, as he headed back to Joseph's that afternoon with Sophie, mute witness to his ordeal, he had cursed his own fame; vowed, "Never again"; even stuck to that resolve, until he met Paul, who unlike the young man in the park was guileless, adoring, sexually enthusiastic, and fueled by a reverence so undiluted it was bracing.

Would that last, however? Kennington wasn't sure. He wasn't even sure whether Paul, whose proclamations of love tended to be so bold and non-sequiturial, knew his own mind, or had merely confused eros with worship, a common sleight of hand in one so young and ambitious. And the degree of his ambition was frightening.

This was becoming clearer to Kennington every day. Lying in bed together that morning, for example, their talk had drifted to record covers, and then to the recording industry in general. Then with a surprising modesty, Paul had announced that his goal was to release his own first CD before he turned twenty-one. Already he'd decided for which company he wanted to record (Deutsche Grammophon or Teldec); the program he would select (Chopin and Debussy études); even what the cover ought to depict (himself in a tuxedo, posed before the Golden Gate Bridge). All of which was fine; day-dream, fantasy, was fine. And yet the extent to which Paul seemed to be devoted to this fantasy also obscured, for Kennington, any clear sense of whether he was also devoted to music itself. For what would happen if he *didn't* make his first CD before he turned twenty-one? And if he did, what would he do when confronted with those horrors that lurk on the other side of arrival? These horrors Kennington knew all too well. Yet he shrunk from explaining to Paul that success could feel as bankrupt as failure, for fear that if he did so, Paul would accuse him of arrogance, having never known failure — at least as the world defines it — himself.

The risk inherent in such single-minded devotion to success as Paul exhibited, Kennington concluded then, was that it could so easily flip-flop into an equally single-minded devotion to failure. This he had seen happen too many times. In his universe there orbited various odd satellites, former prodigies who had never quite managed the transition out of childhood, and forgotten competition winners playing recitals to half-empty houses, and teachers at obscure music schools who made careers out of Ravel's *Concerto for the Left Hand* because they had maimed themselves trying to play like Horowitz in their youth. Most were socially inept; many were pickled in drink. Kennington wished he could show these people to Paul; and he also wished he could prove to his young friend the vacuity of the notion that this polarity of success/failure must form the backbone of any artist's life. The truth is, it must not — and yet how hard to resist the siren scream insisting otherwise!

So he ruminated. At times Paul drove him so crazy with questions that he wanted to break off with him altogether. At other times he longed for the boy with an intensity that resulted in him saying and doing all sorts of things he later regretted: suggesting, for instance, that maybe he'd go with him and his mother to Florence, or allowing a conversation in which each of them was building a dream house to verge into a conversation in which they were building a dream house together. This sort of game was unwise, especially when you were playing it with an eighteen-year-old who has not yet learned to distinguish the fancy of the moment from the truth of all time. Still, for his own pleasure, he kept giving in. There was more than a touch of sadism in his surrenders. Also love.

And that was the greatest mystery of all: how to account for the sensation of uncorrupted, even childish joy that intermittently stole upon him in Paul's company. One night he hadn't been able to sleep from the intoxication of it, and rising from his bed, had walked the empty city, across bridges and through alleys over which laundry swayed, until at dawn he found himself witnessing a sylvan scene: a group of eight boys — provincials, probably, in for a night at the discos — shaving and brushing their teeth at one of those public water spigots that punctuate the Roman landscape. Each had an Invicta backpack, from which he extracted a clean white towel, a toothbrush, a cake of soap. Together, as Kennington had never been together with other boys: he could have watched them for hours.

Another of his evenings with Paul and Pamela: not yet sleepy after dinner, the three of them had gone to see *West Side Story* at an English-language movie theater in Trastevere. Through narrow streets they had hurried, until they reached the Pasquino, which was located off a vine-covered alley. Most of the seats were broken. The paint was peeling off the walls, which gave off an odor of wet dog. Initially there was some tension about the seating arrangements, which resolved itself only when Kennington sat in the middle, Pamela on one side of him, Paul on the other. Paul took his hand. He could feel the fine antennae of Pamela's blouse brushing against his arm. The movie started. At first he had trouble concentrating. But then he relaxed into the warmth of it, the easy familiarity of it. They watched peacefully until, in the middle of "America," the film broke, the lights went up, a hand pulled away from his own. "It's hot," Paul said, rolling up his sleeves as the old man who had taken their tickets emerged through a door in the screen bearing a tray of melting chocolate bars. *"Bonbons di gela',"* he incanted. *"Bonbons di gela'. Acqua, coca, aranciata."*

The movie started up again. From her side Pamela pressed closer. It was halfway through "I Have a Love" that the wrenching noises started — like gears being forced, Paul would later say. "What's that?" Pamela whispered.

"I don't know." And then a breeze was freshening the fetid theater. "Look!" Paul said. "Look up!"

Kennington did. The ceiling was parting in two, the spreading aperture revealing a band of stars: some primitive form of air conditioning.

Haltingly the noise of gears continued. The sky widened. It was purple and smoke gray, and Kennington was thinking how much it resembled the chalkboards in his elementary school, when a screech sounded, and something fell: all at once a cat was sitting on his lap, perfectly poised, its eyes lurid in the gloaming.

For a nanosecond he and the cat gazed at each other. Then it hissed, rearranged its legs, and disappeared into the outer darkness.

They did not laugh. Instead the stillness of amazement claimed them as Marni Nixon sang through Natalie Wood's lips, and a plane passed across the moonlit sky: a streak of light so fine it might have been meant to underline some message written on that chalkboard of an evening. At that moment, however, none of them could have said what the message was.

# 9

TUSHI'S YOUNG MAN was bored. He had been sitting for close to an hour in Joseph Mansourian's living room, playing Tetris while his lady love gave succor behind closed doors. Not that he minded waiting; indeed, Tushi's indispensability to her friends was one of the traits he found most admirable in her. The trouble was that tonight they had a nine o'clock reservation at a restaurant where you had to book two weeks in advance. If she took too much longer, the young man realized, they might miss the reservation entirely, which would be a shame, as he was currently in the midst of his internship at Mount Sinai and therefore obliged to eat more dinners at the hospital cafeteria than he cared to.

To distract himself, he got up from the leather sofa where he had been stationed. Joseph's living room was generously proportioned, with crown moldings and high ceilings. The floors were of polished parquet, overlaid with Persian rugs. Behind double-swag curtains Central Park spread out in all its verdant amplitude. A little alcove where Joseph kept his CD and record collection fronted the piano, which the young man, not able to play himself, now approached with some timidity. Photographs were arranged atop the lid, most of them featuring a long-haired dachshund and a short-haired man at various stages in their growth. The latter he took to be Kennington: Kennington, the source of Joseph's tribulations, and their emergency visit. According to Tushi, Joseph and Kennington had been together for more than twenty years, even though they never had sex anymore, and both of them slept with other men. She knew. Over time, they had both gotten into the habit of confessing to her, so that she needed constantly to keep track of what was a secret and what was not.

Abandoning the piano, the young man returned to the sofa, where he flipped through a copy of *New York*. To his chagrin, he was starting to feel a little exasperated, a little — well — miffed. Love troubles, of course, he understood: he'd had his own. Even so, when he was having love troubles, it had never occured to *him* to summon a friend to his bedside. Instead he'd simply gotten drunk and watched *Nick at Nite*. And this, in his view, was the right, the proper, course of action. Joseph's behavior, on the other hand, did seem to him (dare he say it?) typically homosexual: an ignorant assessment, Tushi would have chided, given that up until now his experience of homosexuals had been pretty much limited to the emergency room, where once he had treated a guy with a lemon stuck in his rectum. When the young man had asked how the lemon had gotten there, the guy had replied, "I fell on it in the shower." Life really was a mysterious and wonderful business.

A door opened. "Sweetheart, I'm so sorry," Tushi said, hurrying toward him. "Joseph's in a terrible state. It took forever to calm him down."

"Don't worry, I'm endlessly resourceful." (Did that sound resentful?)

"You have the patience of a saint." Tushi embraced him. "Well, we'd better get going."

"I hope he's okay." The young man picked up her coat and kissed her forehead.

"He'll make it through, I think. I promised I'd call in the morning. Help me on with it, will you?"

He did, after which they headed out the door to the hall. "Free at last," she said as they rode down in the elevator, and she kissed him back. "Oh my darling, how lucky I am to have you!"

"How lucky I am," the young man echoed. Then they walked through the foyer to the sidewalk, where the doorman hailed them a cab.

It was raining a little. Riding downtown, Tushi traced the progress of water down the window with her finger. Of course, the young man was dying to ask her what had happened. Only the desire not to seem nosy held him back.

"The middle age of buggers is not to be contemplated without horror," she said after a moment.

*"What?"*

"Virginia Woolf, from her diaries. Don't worry, *I* didn't write it." She took a tissue from her purse. "Still, I'm inclined to agree. I mean, doesn't it all seem rather tragic? They reach fifty, and suddenly they start collecting saltcellars, or breeding Dandie Dinmont terriers. Anything to ease the loneliness."

"Is that Joseph's problem? Loneliness?"

"I've always believed that childlessness is biology's revenge on homosexuals."

"But Joseph's not alone. He has that boyfriend."

"Who makes him suffer more than anyone."

"Why? What's he done?"

"Nothing very unusual, so far as I can tell. He's in Rome, and won't say when he's coming back. And he's refusing to answer Joseph's faxes. Also, he never showed up at some tony official dinner, and hasn't called to commiserate over Sophie's — the dachshund's — death. From all of which Joseph concludes that he must be having an affair."

"Why?"

"It's a pattern that goes back years. They've been together since Richard was very young, a boy, practically. You know Richard's father abandoned his mother when he was a baby. And it's bound to get worse before it gets better, isn't it? After all, Richard's about to turn forty. It's the age where you become terrified of missing out before your youth is over. Whereas poor Joseph's at that age where you're frightened of growing old alone." She pulled her hair back over her ears. "I keep telling him he should move on, find someone he's more suited to, but he won't hear of it. He says he can't imagine life without Richard."

"Even if they don't have sex?"

"Sex, my darling, is often the least important part of a passion. You'll learn that when you get older."

The young man was silent. He didn't like to be reminded of the difference in their ages.

They arrived at the restaurant. "Well, isn't this lovely," Tushi said a bit cynically, gazing at a fountain that rose up in the middle of the room.

"Lovely," the young man repeated. Then they sat down, and he said, "Tushi, do you ever worry about my being so much younger than you are?"

"Of course."

"And yet I can't imagine *us* ever ending up in a situation like Joseph's."

"What, you mean with me keeping a stable of gigolos, and you using it as justification to go to bed with every adoring young woman that comes your way?"

"It's interesting," the young man said, "how automatically you assume Joseph's role."

"Of course I do. I'm the older one." She touched his hand. "But the problem in their case isn't *only* age. Richard's champing at the bit. He wants to be free."

"Whereas I want to be enslaved." He leaned closer.

Smiling, she sipped from her water glass. "What are you telling me, that you'd like me to tie your wrists to the bedposts?"

"I wouldn't mind."

"Well, isn't this interesting." She squeezed his hand. "You really are a filthy little boy."

The waiter brought their menus. As he studied his, the young man tried subtly to rearrange his erection, which was pressing painfully against his thigh. "Ooh, black fettuccine with lobster and fresh peas," Tushi said. "Doesn't that sound good?"

"Wonderful," the young man answered. "Everything with you sounds wonderful."

Under the table, he guided her hand to his erection. She hardly blushed. "Or maybe the spaghetti alla chitarra. Yes, tonight spaghetti alla chitarra might be just the thing."

"You are a terrible woman," he said, and no longer thought of the man they had left behind: the griefs of strangers are easy to ignore. But Tushi did. Even as she pushed and prodded, she thought of Joseph, lying in his bedroom while darkness bled through the window. "Memory banks," he'd said. "What a mysterious phrase that is, as if memory were a river." And so it was on a riverside that she saw him now, his pants rolled up to the ankles, trailing his long legs as he reached down to sift through the silt and sand and mud that was his own history. And what might he dredge up before daybreak? Something that would help him? She hoped so. But she couldn't guess.

# 10

PAUL WAS SITTING NAKED in the armchair in Kennington's hotel room, shower water dripping from his neck into the cleft of his chest. He was staring at Kennington, who was on the bed, reading the *Herald Tribune*.

It unnerved Kennington, the way Paul stared. Periodically he would glance over the serrated edges of his paper, and there they would be: those eyes, always open too wide, like the eyes of a child kept up past its bedtime; and indeed, like a child kept up past its bedtime, something in Paul seemed to be resisting tonight not only the need to rest, but to grow.

Finally Kennington put down the paper. "Paul," he said.

"Yes?"

"Why are you staring at me?"

"Staring at you?"

"That's right."

Quiet. "I guess I'm trying to memorize your face," Paul said. "In case I never see you again."

"And what makes you think you'll never see me again?"

"Well, the day after tomorrow we leave for Florence."

"True."

"And you head back to New York."

"Also true."

"Unless —"

"Unless what?"

"Well, unless you've given any thought to the possibility of coming with us. You mentioned the other day you might."

"Did I?" Kennington returned to his paper. "I must have been in a delirium. Roman fever or something."

"Oh."

"Not that I wouldn't like to. It's just not realistic. After all, I haven't been home in more than a month. The mail in my apartment must be piled up to the ceiling."

"How important is mail?"

"Important enough. Then there's Joseph. His dog's been sick."

"Well, he's only your manager —"

"Plus I have to practice. Remember what Von Bülow said? If you don't practice for one day, you know it. If you don't practice for two days, the critics know it. If you don't practice for three days, the public knows it. As it stands I haven't touched a piano for a week."

There was little Paul could say in response to this observation beyond a slightly peeved "of course." Kennington turned the page.

After a moment Paul stood up and started getting dressed.

"Are you leaving?" Kennington asked from behind his paper.

"We're supposed to meet my mother in half an hour for dinner, unless you've decided that's not realistic, either."

"Okay, okay." Climbing out of bed, Kennington started dressing too. "I can't help but observe that you're not your usual perky self this evening," he said, as they headed out of the hotel and toward Piazza Barberini. "Is something on your mind?"

Paul was silent for a second. Then he said, "I'm sorry, but I'm disappointed about Florence. After all, you're the one who brought it up, and when you did, you sounded so enthusiastic that I assumed you were really serious about it. That after my mother left, maybe we could even travel on together a little bit. Alone together."

"Sounds wonderful."

"But not wonderful enough to do."

Kennington laughed. "Oh, if I had a dollar for every wonderful thing I haven't done!"

"Then why don't you do it? *I'll* give you a dollar."

Kennington shook his head. "Certain patterns are too expensive to break."

"Even for just a few days?"

They were waiting for a green light, Paul gazing at him imploringly.

Then the light changed. They moved on.

"So what happens next?" Paul asked.

"Next? I go back to New York. You go to Florence. And in the fall you'll start at Juilliard."

"And will we see each other?"

"Of course we'll see each other."

"But yesterday you said you'd be away most of the fall. You said you had to go to Germany in October, then Japan —"

"For me that's nothing. I'll be home a lot more than I usually am, and when I'm there we can see each other all the time."

"But you haven't even given me your phone number."

"That's only because I'm almost never there. It's better if I call you —"

"I hate this," Paul said suddenly. "The way you're describing it, you get your tour, and your apartment, and you don't go to Florence, and you get me whenever you call. Whereas I get nothing."

"Is that what you're in this for? To get something?"

Paul didn't answer. A car roared down the narrow street, forcing them up against the wall.

They continued walking.

"So will Mr. Mansourian go with you to Germany?" Paul asked after a few seconds.

"No. He doesn't usually travel with me these days. San Francisco was an exception."

"He *is* a homosexual, isn't he?"

"Yes. Why do you ask?"

"Because of the way he acted toward me in San Francisco."

Kennington twitched a little. "And how did he act toward you in San Francisco?"

"Oh, you know . . . the way you did here."

They had reached the Trevi Fountain, where Paul dug in his pockets. Kennington, quiet, watched the arc of a coin as it spiraled over the green water.

Then they crossed the street and caught a taxi. They had an appointment to meet Pamela at a pizzeria that the Romans called "the morgue" because of its marble tabletops. Alone under fluorescent light she waited for them, looking oddly intimidated in her new pink Valentino suit. From the ovens one of the *pizzaioli,* his T-shirt smeared with tomato, stared at her, while nearer by the pretty girl at the cash register was wearing the same Valentino suit, albeit in green instead of pink. Along with what looked like a pound of gold.

"Sorry we're late," Kennington said, kissing Pamela on the cheek as he sat down.

"Oh, don't worry. I've been having a wonderful time, watching those chefs throw that dough." She clasped her hands under her chin. "Pizza making really is an art, isn't it?"

"Roman pizza's the thin-crusted kind," Paul said. "It's thicker in Naples."

A waiter, unsmiling, dropped menus on the table. "Oh my," Pamela said, scanning the choices. "You know, Richard, pizza's just about my favorite food in the world. Did Paul tell you?"

"No."

"And now to be having a genuine Roman pizza in a genuine Roman pizzeria — it's just thrilling!" She returned her gaze to the menu. "Now let's see . . . mushroom sounds good. And what's a Napoli?"

"Mozzarella and anchovies, I think."

"I don't like anchovies. Maybe mushroom then. Or sausage. Or what's this? My goodness, zucchini flowers. How exotic!"

"*Prego,*" the waiter said, returning.

They ordered, Pamela opting for the zucchini flowers. The waiter went away.

A silence immediately fell over their table, mostly because the mob of German women across the way was talking so loudly. Also, each of them was watching something: Paul, Kennington; Pamela (alternately) the *pizzaiolo* and Kennington; Kennington, a handsome boy who stood behind a butcher-block counter in the open kitchen. Taking a sharp knife, the boy spread his left hand out on the butcher block and stabbed at the wood between his fingers, moving from the space between thumb and index finger to the space between index and middle finger to the space between middle and ring finger to the space between ring finger and pinkie, then back again. He did it so fast the steel blade blurred: five, six times. Then he stopped, breathed, started again, as if he were trying to break his own record.

Their drinks arrived: Nastro Azzurro for Kennington, water for Pamela and Paul. Kennington's expression, as he watched the boy, was avid, almost lustful. And what was he hoping for? Paul wondered. That the boy might make a mistake, chop off a finger or a fingertip? That he wouldn't make a mistake, and prove his mettle? All that was obvious was that if this was a game, the boy was winning it; time after time he won it.

Soon their pizzas arrived, spilling over the edges of plates too small to contain them.

"Oh my, isn't this beautiful?" said Pamela, looking first at her son and then his friend. "So beautiful I almost can't bear to eat it."

Tears welled in her eyes — tears that neither Kennington nor Paul noticed, so quickly did she cough them back. "Well, *buon appetito,*" she said.

"*Buon appetito,*" they repeated in unison.

She took a bite, a little nervously, having never eaten flowers before. But as it turned out, they were delicious.

# 11

THEIR LAST MORNING in Rome, Kennington was supposed to go with Paul and his mother to Tivoli, to see the Villa d'Este. Indeed, at nine Paul was already dressed and ready in his room, when the phone rang. "Good morning," Kennington said. "Did you sleep well?"

"Not really. Richard, about our conversation last night — I feel that I owe you —"

"Nonsense. If anyone owes anyone an apology it's me." He sneezed.

"Are you all right?"

"No. Actually, that's the reason I'm calling. I think I'm catching a cold."

"Oh?"

"Nothing serious. Only I'm not sure I'm up to an expedition today. Would you mind terribly if I bagged out?"

"Of course not." Paul's voice grew chilly. "You're free to do whatever you want. You know that."

"Well, if you really wouldn't mind, as things stand I think I'd probably rather rest this morning. I'm sure I'll feel better in the afternoon, and then we can meet as usual at the Bar della Pace. How does that sound?"

"Fine," Paul said.

"You have fun now, you hear?"

"I will."

"I'll miss you."

"Thank you. I'll miss you too."

They hung up. Picking up his backpack, Paul stomped downstairs to his mother's room. "Are you ready?" he shouted, rapping on the door.

"Almost. Come in!"

He barreled through and hurled himself onto the bed. Pamela was doing her make-up. "Sleep well?" she asked.

"Richard isn't coming," he answered matter-of-factly. "He says he has a cold."

Pamela colored. "You know, that's funny, Paul" — she put down her lipstick — "because as it happens my allergies are acting up this morning. Would you mind —"

"Oh, so now I'm supposed to go alone?"

"Well, you're always saying you need time to yourself, honey."

He rolled onto his side. "All right." Hoisting himself up from the bed, he headed for the door. "Well, bye."

"Bye, sweetheart. Be careful. See you this afternoon, okay?"

"Fine."

"You have enough money?"

"Yes."

The door slammed shut. Turning around, Pamela examined herself in the mirror; she looked good enough, she decided. Next, making sure first that the coast was clear, she hurried downstairs and across the street to a little grocery store, where she bought orange juice, pretzels, and a package of *cornetti*. At the pharmacy she got vitamin C tablets. Finally, on the Corso Vittorio Emanuele, she hailed a cab. "Hotel Bristol," she said, adjusting her collar as the driver moved her into traffic.

It occurred to her that what she was doing was very possibly mad. And yet might not this announcement of illness also encode the clue for which she'd been waiting, delivered shyly — or perhaps slyly — through Paul?

No one stopped her — indeed, no one noticed her — in the Bristol lobby. Relieved not to have been accused of prostitution, she rode the elevator to the sixth floor, feeling rather conspicuous with her sack of groceries. Down the long corridor she walked, past open doors and metal carts loaded with linens and little shampoo bottles, until she reached the room she knew to be Kennington's, the room marked 611.

She knocked. *"Chi è?"* a voice asked from inside.

"Pamela."

Silence. Several seconds passed before Kennington opened the door. Unshaven, he stood lumpishly before her, in gray sweatpants and a Tanglewood T-shirt.

"Hi," he said.

"Hi," she said. "I hope I'm not interrupting."

"No, not at all. Come in."

He stepped aside to let her pass. His room, though elegant, was a mess: the bed unmade, a shirt draped over the back of a chair.

"This is lovely," she said, putting down her bag. "So refined."

Hugging her arms, she grinned at him.

Silence.

"Well, I'll bet you're surprised to see me, aren't you?"

"Yes, in fact. I assumed you'd gone with Paul to Tivoli."

"Oh, at the last minute I decided to stay. I wasn't really in the mood for a bus ride."

"Ah."

"And then when Paul told me you weren't feeling well, I thought, I'll bring him some breakfast. Here." She handed him the bag. "I've got orange juice, pretzels, croissants. Something sweet and something salty, that's what Paul always likes when he's sick. Also, vitamin C."

"Thanks." Kennington put the bag down on the dresser. "You really didn't have to go to all this trouble."

"Oh, but I wanted to. Especially after all the meals you've bought us."

"But it was my pleasure."

"Well, now it's my turn to be hospitable. So you just lie down over there" — she pointed to the bed — "and I'll get breakfast ready. Do you have any glasses?"

"Over by the minibar."

"I'll get them. You stay put."

She took two tumblers from a shelf, poured the juice, handed him a glass.

"*Cin-cin.*"

"It's bad luck to toast with anything other than wine."

"Oh, I didn't know."

"Let me clear that off for you," he added, getting up and removing the shirt from the chair.

She sat, and Kennington returned to the bed, where he lay down and crossed his legs at the ankles.

"So," Pamela said, smiling loudly. (What to say now?) "Actually, Richard, I do have a little confession to make. I didn't come by your room this morning *only* to bring you orange juice."

"You didn't."

She shook her head. "The truth is, I had an ulterior motive. In fact, I only decided not to go to Tivoli after Paul told me you weren't coming. Was that wicked of me?"

"Why would it be wicked?"

"Because, well, to be honest, I wanted you all to myself." She laughed. "And please don't assume from that that I haven't enjoyed the time the three of us spent together. I have. It's just that, do you realize this whole week you and I haven't had a single minute by ourselves? Without Paul?"

"No, I guess not."

"Have a croissant," she added, getting up and ripping into the package.

Crumbs fell into the sheets as he tore the somewhat stale croissant in half.

"How is it?"

"Oh, delicious."

"Good. You want some pretzels?"

"No thanks. Not just yet."

"You can keep them in case you have a craving." She sat down again, wrapped her hands one around the other. "You know, Richard, I've been wanting to tell you how grateful I am to you for all the help you've given Paul and me on this trip. I mean, when we arrived, as you could see, I was a wreck. And now look at me."

"I'm glad you're feeling better. Still, I can't take credit."

"Oh, but you should! If today I can face things again, it's thanks to you." She leaned into the soft, embracing fabric of the armchair. "A bad marriage can be a very ego-draining thing. You assume that just because there's no love, then no one can love you."

"I understand."

All at once she spilled out the saga of Kelso's abandonment, with which of course Kennington was already familiar.

"And yet it never occurred to me to get out of it," she concluded, "because it's all so familiar, that kind of misery, so . . . homey, almost. You see what I'm saying? It's funny. At first I was angry at Kelso. But now I feel almost grateful to him. After all, if he'd come with us to Rome . . ." Her voice fell away.

"It's a decision I suspect he'll live to regret," Kennington answered after some seconds.

"You're sweet to tell me that. And I can't deny that deep down, I probably do hope his little liaison turns out to be a failure. You know, that he comes over, begs me to take him back, and I basically say, 'Up yours.'" She covered her teeth with her hand. "Isn't that horrible of me to say?"

"I don't think it's horrible at all. I think it's natural."

"I'm happy to hear it. I trust your judgment. So does Paul."

"Does he?"

"You're his hero, Richard. Why, I can remember taking him to buy his first record. He couldn't have been more than nine. And he'd been saving his allowance for weeks, and finally, when he had enough, I drove him to the record store, which was this very sixties place, basically a huge wooden box on the edge of El Camino Real — we always just called it 'The Box' — and I watched as he walked over to the classical section, so proud, and thumbed through the albums until he found your new one, and made all these meticulous comparisons between the copies until he decided which one was perfect. Then he carried it over to the counter and bought it with change. All change." She laughed. "That's why this trip has meant so much to him. Why, just think, if those gypsy girls hadn't attacked me, if you hadn't happened to be in the piazza at the same instant . . ."

"And tomorrow you're off to Florence. Are you excited?"

"Let's not talk about that. Would you like some more juice?"

"No, I'm fine."

"How about some vitamin C? Oh, I'm so scatterbrained, I haven't even asked how you're feeling."

"Congested. Also, my throat hurts."

"Any fever? Let me feel your head."

"I haven't got a fever."

Moving to sit next to him on the bed, she cupped her cool palm against his brow. "No, you're not warm."

"I told you, I haven't got a fever."

She did not remove her hand.

"Pamela —"

Still she did not remove her hand.

A panicked virago, she smiled: all teeth.

Some time passed very slowly. "You know what?" Pamela said after a while. "Maybe you do just have the tiniest bit of temperature. I'll go and get you a wet cloth."

Taking away her hand (it was hot now), she retreated to the bathroom, where very delicately she closed the door, switched on the tap, picked out a facecloth. Cream-colored, this facecloth. Plush. She stared at it until her vision blurred. Then she sat down on the toilet, and for just a few seconds buried her face in the cloth, heaved breath, formed her hands into fists.

For some reason an old memory assailed her. Taking a French course in college once, she had studied so hard for her midterm that she'd ended up mismemorizing a key rule of grammar, and getting an F. Yet when she explained what had happened, her professor had shown little sympathy. "No ear!" he'd said, tapping her on the side of the head.

*No ear.*

"Fool," she whispered to herself, "idiot," until, realizing that she could not sit like that all morning, she got up again; checked her make-up, which seemed to be all right; wet and wrung out the facecloth. Indeed, she was just about ready to go out again, when she noticed a pair of boxer shorts hanging on the back of the door. They were pale blue, from Brooks Brothers, just like the ones she'd given Paul last Christmas.

Moving closer, she plucked the boxers from their hook. They were torn down the middle seam.

*Were* they Paul's? The label was the same, the size the same. And yet if they were Paul's, what were they doing in Kennington's bathroom? Maybe Kennington owned an identical pair. Not unlikely. But the same size?

Putting them back where she'd found them, she opened the door. Kennington was still lying where she'd left him.

"Here," she said, handing him the cloth. "This should make you feel better."

"Thanks." He pressed it against his forehead.

"I always made these up for my kids when they were sick. They really eat the fever." With her left hand she rubbed at what seemed to be a sore spot on the back of her head.

Kennington closed his eyes, let the moisture soak into his brow.

"Well, I should probably skedaddle," she said after a minute. "You need to rest."

"Yes, I think a little sleep will do me a world of good."

"So, I'll see you this afternoon at the caffè, how about that? Unless —" She raised her head proudly. "Well, I guess I just want to say that if you don't feel up to meeting us this afternoon, you shouldn't feel obligated, Richard. At least not on our account."

"Oh, I don't," Kennington answered quickly. "In fact, I'm

sure after a little sleep I'll be" — he snapped his fingers — "fit as a fiddle."

"Good," Pamela said, feeling sacrificial. "That'll mean a lot to Paul."

She held out her hand toward the bed, but Kennington was already on his feet, moving toward the door, holding it open for her to pass through.

Once Pamela had gone, Kennington immediately bolted the door behind him. During the course of her visit, he noticed, the bellhop had slipped through another fax. He picked it up and was about to stuff it, as he had the others, into the bedside drawer, when a familiar name leapt out at him. Alarmed, he read the fax through. Then he opened the drawer and dragged out the other faxes, and read those through as well. To his regret and horror, he discovered that Joseph had never once mentioned Signore Batisti, but wrote only of Sophie, whose death, it seemed, had crushed his spirit more ferociously than Kennington would have thought possible.

He picked up the phone and dialed. "It's me," he told Joseph's voice mail. "Joseph, I am so sorry about Sophie. Please call me back. I . . . I don't know what else to say." Then he hung up and sat down on the bed. Five minutes passed. He picked up the phone and tried Joseph's number a second time. Again the voice mail answered. He didn't leave a message.

Getting up, he took off his clothes. That he had to get away — a possibility already brewing in his head for several days — he now felt certain. No, he should never have suggested, even casually, accompanying them to Florence for now not only Paul, but his mother was in love with him. Everything, as usual, had gone too far too fast (his own fault) so that from the very intensity of the affair — the habit pleasure has of curling up hotly at the edges — he found himself wanting to run. It was more than he could handle, more than he wanted to handle. For if he continued with Paul, what would welcome him but problems? From Pamela there would be wrath to contend with; from Paul himself, competitiveness or envy. Or perhaps he would try to use Kennington's fame to jump-start his own career, or resent that fame as an impediment. It was possible. Anything was possible.

As for Joseph, *could* they even separate? They were joined by more than need. Their money was as intertwined as two lovers waking on a winter morning. Which meant that if they did break up, the resulting turmoil would be financial as well as emotional; even, perhaps, public; no, it was more than he could bear to contemplate.

He pulled on his jeans. He was, he recognized, having a panic attack; and though he could now hold his panic at a distance, as it were, examine it — he was one of those people who at moments of crisis gain access to a certain clarity, even tranquillity of intention — still, panic alone ran in his nerves.

Had Paul found his phone number? He hoped not. Even so, to be on the safe side, he'd be sure to change it when he got back.

It wouldn't be the first time he'd changed his number.

He picked up the telephone, called Delta, and arranged to

switch his reservation onto the flight that departed the next morning (easy, because he was traveling first-class). Then he called the front desk and explained that due to an emergency he would have to be checking out immediately. Then he called Joseph and left a second message, this one more restrained, telling him when he'd be home.

Phone calls finished, he packed, which took no time at all; after so many years of travel, he could get his luggage together in ten minutes flat. Finally he checked under the bed and in the bathroom, where he discovered Paul's torn boxer shorts hanging on the back of the door. Had Pamela seen them? he wondered.

Did it matter? Not anymore.

Picking them up, he held the boxer shorts to his nose, for an instant; for an instant, breathed Paul's stale, sweet smell. Then he dropped them into the trash can.

A taxi picked him up outside the hotel. Through a dry, dreary zone of high-rise apartment blocks and empty lots he rode, past the Baths of Caracalla to EUR, its fascistic towers gleaming whitely in the hot noon light. The landscape of this part of the city had a lunar aspect that would have frightened Kennington if it hadn't seemed so transitional, so impermanent. And how urgently, at that moment, he longed for his loft, for his piano, for familiar things: sheets and pillows he knew, and Joseph's apartment, and the sofa with its smell of leather and dachshund, through which just the slightest note of honey always seemed to rise! All the things he feared losing, if he left Joseph. Even Joseph himself. Yet home had its own evils, too. Perhaps best of all, then, these waterless seas, where no one could find him.

In his room at the Sheraton, near Fiumicino, he did not unpack. Instead he sat on the edge of the bed, gazing out the window at the cars on their way to the airport. Their progress had a curiously tranquilizing effect on him. Indeed, even the room itself, so coldly functional after the overstuffed Bristol, seemed to radiate a dull, impersonal sense of possibility that calmed Kennington: the architectural equivalent of a blank page. Nor would anyone be able to track him down here. Of course Paul might try his little trick of going through the hotel listings in the yellow pages; and yet somehow Kennington doubted that even Paul would guess where he'd come.

Tomorrow, he thought. Home. Home to Joseph.

And would he ever meet the Porterfields again? Run into Paul at Lincoln Center? Stumble up against Pamela outside the opera house in San Francisco? Right now Paul was probably still at Tivoli. And Pamela . . . she was probably at the Bernini, reading or weeping. Looking forward to Paul coming home, at which point they would head over to the Bar della Pace, wait for him fifteen minutes, half an hour . . .

Then what would they do?

He didn't want to guess.

The next day Kennington boarded a plane for New York, while Paul and his mother caught a morning train to Florence.

# MUSICLAND

# 12
_____

"IF YOU'RE NOT even going to make an effort, I don't see what the point is," Bobby Newman told Teddy Moss, getting up from between his knees.

Over the smooth edge of *The Wall Street Journal* he was reading (paper sharp enough to draw blood), Teddy watched impassively while his friend pulled on white underpants.

"Whatever," he said. Then he stubbed out a cigar in the ashtray and returned to his article, which concerned certain recent advancements in the fiber optics industry.

"What are you doing that for?"

"I hate cigars. I was only smoking it, or pretending to smoke it, for your sake."

"Oh, that's great. That really makes my day." Bobby was nearly trembling with fury, which Teddy found funny. Also, Bobby knew Teddy found his fury funny. This was the worst part. He could have picked up the ashtray and thrown it against the wall, except probably it wouldn't have broken. (There was a dull bruise near the window where he'd thrown it once before.) Also, if he did throw the ashtray, he knew, Teddy's bemusement would very likely transform instantly into mute and focused rage. "That's it," he'd say, pick Bobby up and heave him out the door, just like the ashtray. Such brutal and efficient silences were what Bobby loved best in Teddy, and gazing at his friend's languorous half erection bobbing below newsprint, he became once again amorous, aroused. "Teddy," he said.

Teddy peered at him over his newspaper.

"Can I —"

"It was your idea. Don't blame me if you bit off more than you can chew."

"I'm sorry I got so huffy. I just felt ignored."

"You wanted to be ignored. You said, and I quote, 'Let me suck you off while you read *The Wall Street Journal*. Pretend you don't even notice I'm doing it.'"

"Yes, *pretend*. But I got the feeling you actually *didn't* notice."

"The article was interesting."

"I guess I'm not sure what I want," Bobby said. "I'm only nineteen." Pulling his underpants off again, he curled in a fetal position between Teddy's knees and held his cock as if it were a microphone.

"Talk about biting off more than you can chew," he said.

"Pretty interesting," Teddy said. "Apple stock has gone down three-eighths."

Bobby made a guttural noise.

A few minutes later, the phone rang.

"Hello?" Teddy said, picking up.

"Teddy? It's Mrs. Porterfield."

"Oh, hi, Mrs. Porterfield, how are you?"

"Oh, well, you know. The divorce and all. But I do what I can to get through the day."

"That's too bad."

"By the way, I saw your mother in the supermarket this morning. We had a little chat. She can't wait to see you at Christmas." A pause. "And is Paolino about, perchance?"

"No, he's at school, practicing."

"Of course! Always practicing. I never seem to catch him at home."

"I can take a message if you want."

"Just tell him I called. I . . . well, to be honest, Teddy, sometimes I think I call too much. I worry it bothers him. What do you think? Do you think it bothers him?"

"I really couldn't speak for Paul, Mrs. Porterfield."

"No, of course not. Well, in any event, your mom and I agreed, it'll be wonderful having you boys home for Christmas. When are you coming?"

"Soon." (He winked at Bobby.)

"What was that?"

"The twentieth! Yes, the twentieth."

"Oh, Pablo's coming the twenty-first. And when are you going back to New York?"

"Third of January."

"I sure am jealous! Your mom gets you for four more days than I get Pauly. Oh well. It's been lovely chatting with you, Teddy. And do let Paolo know I called."

"Will do."

"Bye-bye."

"Bye."

He hung up.

"Your roommate's mother?" Bobby asked, getting up to wash his hands.

There was no reply.

"I always wonder whether he really exists."

"He does."

"Do I ever get to meet him? Is he cute?"

"Not your type. Anyway, I told you, he's always practicing. He's a pianist."

"Oh yeah, with some big-shot lover in the theater world, isn't that right?"

"It's supposed to be a secret. I'm not supposed to say who it is."

"Doesn't matter. I don't know anything about theater." Kissing Teddy, Bobby grimaced. "Yuck, you taste like cigar. Brush your teeth."

"Fuck you," Teddy said. "It was only because you asked me." But he went to the kitchen sink and brushed his teeth anyway.

When Paul arrived an hour later to pick up his mail, Teddy and Bobby were already gone. In their wake a heavy odor of sex suffused the air: sweat and mouthwash and . . . but what *was* that peculiar stench, that almost sugary bitterness, like burnt chestnuts? Oh, a cigar: still wet at the tip, it stood shoved headfirst into its embers like a dark and stubby phallus. From the sofa, the interleaved pages of a *Wall Street*

*Journal* cascaded onto the floor. Paul picked them up. Underneath was a white sock. Teddy never wore white socks. And who'd brought *The Wall Street Journal* into the apartment? Teddy only read *The Village Voice*. The owner of the white sock, no doubt. As it was none of his business, he dropped the pages of the newspaper where he'd found them.

His room was a haven of neatness in the rather unkempt apartment. Amid the carefully arranged implements on the desk — pens and pencils in a jar, legal pad, Liquid Paper in white and yellow, a Scotch tape dispenser — Teddy had left Paul's mail: two letters from his mother, one from his father, and a Steinway circular. He opened his father's letter first. In it, Kelso explained facts of which Pamela, by phone, had already apprised him: as soon as the divorce came through, he and Muriel Peete were getting married. "I hope you will have lunch with us when you're home for Xmas," Kelso wrote,

> though if you prefer not to we understand. And Muriel wants you to know that she never expects to be a substitute mother for you just as she would never expect me to be a substitute father for her Stewart who is yr. age.

At the bottom, in a rather feverish hand, Muriel had added, "Can't wait to meet you, Paul!" and drawn a Santa Claus face.

After folding up his father's letter, Paul opened the first of his mother's. "Menlo Park," he read in the top righthand corner, "4:12 A.M."

That was all he needed to know. He slid the letter back into its envelope, then put a CD on his old stereo — it was Kennington's debut (Chopin préludes) — switched off the light, and lay down on the hard little bed. Some previous occupant of the apartment had pasted glow-in-the-dark stars on the ceiling. Now a greenish firmament spread out above him: constellations and planets, comets, nebulae and sprays of tiny stars. This private universe was something Paul would have liked to share with Alden Haynes, his lover of the past two months, except that Alden had never once come up and spent the night with him. Oh, Paul asked him sometimes — requests Alden always greeted with friendly laughter. What was the point, his laughter implied, when his own place was so much more comfortable? And Paul had to agree, Alden's seven-room co-op on Central Park West *was* more comfortable. So they slept every night in that immense bed with its ecru sheets, that bed from the ample widths of which the treetops of Central Park could be viewed, but where the ceiling held no stars. Comfort and luxury. Paul liked Alden; hoped, suspected, dreaded he might spend years with Alden, until one or the other of them died. At first that bed had seemed the hot navel of the world. But now they lay side by side most nights reading, Alden's half-glasses slipping off his nose, while the lamp buzzed like a mosquito. "I'll have to get that fixed," he always said, sounding for all the world like Paul's own father. And would Kennington, with whom he had once watched a Roman sky open, have appreciated his ceilingful of stars?

Keys sounded in the lock. Getting up and lowering the

volume on the stereo, Paul peered through the door into the living room, where Teddy was unwinding his scarf.

"How's it going?" Teddy asked, smiling his best Optimists' Club smile.

"Not bad." Paul emerged fully from the dark. "I just came by to check my mail."

Opening a can of Diet Coke, Teddy sat down on the sofa. "Your mother called this afternoon. It was pretty funny, the whole time we were talking I was getting a blow job." With his left hand he fingered the cigar butt. "It's probably none of my business . . . still, I thought I ought to tell you. She doesn't sound good."

"She isn't." Paul sat down across from him. "By the way, I finished *Maurice*. Thanks for loaning it to me."

"What did you think?"

"I liked everything except the ending. Probably I'm skeptical, but the fact that you never get to hear what actually happens to Maurice and Alec after they run away together doesn't sit well with me. Besides, what *is* a greenwood?"

"Let's look it up, shall we?" And getting up, Teddy pulled his *American Heritage Dictionary* from the shelf. "'Greenwood,'" he read, scrolling with his finger. "'A wood or forest with green foliage.'" He shut the dictionary. "Actually, according to my professor, it comes from Edward Carpenter. He was this queer philosopher who basically left the world and went off with his lover George Merrill to be woodcutters together."

"Left the world? Is that possible?"

"Maybe then. But it doesn't matter, my professor says, because for men of Forster's generation the greenwood was a hypothetical gay-positive space they had to posit in order to will into being." Smiling, he stuck out his tongue, then went off to his room to study.

"A hypothetical gay-positive space," Paul repeated to himself as he rode downtown on the subway. It occurred to him that until recently he'd thought of Alden Haynes's apartment as a kind of greenwood, a place defined by its opposition to the world, from which it brooked no trespass. But was it, really? The conclusions of most stories, he decided, were probably lies, except in the case of biographies, which end the way lives do: in death. For greenwoods die too. The world encroaches upon them, or there are encroachments from within. What happens when, as months pass (there must be a house or hut, a primitive kitchen), the boiling liquid of new love thickens and cools? Becomes, in effect, a preserve? (What else is marriage?) Paul thought the metaphor of jam-making apposite, since this was a domestic story — albeit one rarely told when the protagonists were both men.

At Alden's building, the doorman with the glossy black hair greeted Paul jovially. Fabric braids glinted on his shoulders as he pushed the revolving door. Then a second doorman rang for the elevator, which had a little velvet bench on which Paul sat. (In certain crucial ways he was still a child.) Indeed, he was already sitting, when a man ran into the lobby, and cried, "Wait!" Pulse quickening, Paul pressed the "door open" button. "Thank you," the man said breathlessly, and looked Paul over. "But haven't we met?"

Paul gulped. Of course he recognized Joseph Mansourian, had recognized him from the moment he'd come leaping through the door.

"Yes we have," Paul said. "I'm Paul Porterfield. I turned pages for Richard Kennington in San Francisco last spring."

Joseph snapped his fingers. "Of course! The well-dressed page turner! And what brings you to my building?"

"I didn't know it was your building. I have a friend who lives here."

The elevator reached the sixteenth floor, and the doors slid open. "Sixteen?" Joseph said. "Then your friend must be Alden Haynes."

"That's right."

"Funny that we haven't run into each other. Alden and I go way back. How's Public Theater working out, by the way?"

"Oh, great. He loves it. He's very busy, of course."

"That was quite a coup for Alden. Well, I'd better not hold up the elevator. Call me sometime." He fished in his pocket. "Here's my card."

"Thanks. You already gave it to me."

"I assume, by the way, that you're at Juilliard?"

"First year."

"Everything going all right? Anything I can do to help?"

"Fine. No, nothing, thanks." He cracked his knuckles. "By the way . . . how is Mr. Kennington doing these days?"

"Richard? Oh, terribly well, terribly well. He's in Japan."

"I see. Say hello to him for me, will you?"

"Sure. Tell me your name again?"

"Paul Porterfield."

"Paul Porterfield. I'll remember."

The elevator closed on Paul's face.

He was now standing in Alden's familiar hall, with its gray carpeting. More than two months had passed since that afternoon Alden had picked him up during an intermission at the Met — months over the course of which this hall had become, in its way, as familiar to him as that of his parents' embattled house in Menlo Park. And during those months, he had at last experienced the world. He'd gone to parties and concerts. An important actress had fawned over him; a famous opera singer, slipping him his phone number, had suggested they "keep each other in the wings" — not an uncommon experience in New York when you are young and good-looking, and possess a certain surface panache. As Paul was learning, the short-term attentions of the powerful are cheaper to obtain than he would ever have previously guessed.

Yet he never ran into Kennington. Of course he kept his eyes peeled. Tushi Strauss, who knew Alden from somewhere, came by to say hello once at a restaurant, in the company of a much younger man: she didn't seem to remember Paul. Also the pianist Magda Tanca, with whom Kennington had once made a recording. But not Kennington himself. Thus Paul's surprise at running into Mr. Mansourian. It was as if, over the months since they'd come back from Italy, he'd ceased to believe in Kennington, as if their affair had been merely a travel-induced dream. Now he had to concede its reality, as well as Mr. Mansourian's apparent ignorance of the facts.

Taking out his keys, he let himself into the apartment. "Alden?" he called, for the lights were on in the entrance hall.

"In here!"

Quietly Paul made his way to the living room, where Alden was standing on a leather armchair, a hammer and nails in his right hand. A framed photograph of Norman, his lover of twelve years, was tucked under his arm.

"How are you today?"

"Not bad." Sitting down in the armchair's twin, Paul watched while Alden marked the spot where the nail should go, then rammed it home. In the window, the armchairs, the glow of the fire and reading lamp and wall sconces, seemed superimposed on the dark treetops and blocks of skyline, to which they lent a faint radiance of domestic warmth.

"There," Alden said, climbing down and stepping back to admire the picture, in which Norman, wearing tennis shorts, posed with his racket. "What do you think?"

"Nice."

"That picture's ancient. Norman couldn't have been much older than you." He put the hammer and nails on top of the piano. Alden was a fair-skinned, well-groomed man of forty, a little on the chubby side, and though he went out to dinner as often as Henry James had in his heyday, he rarely if ever invited friends to his apartment. And this, Paul suspected, was chiefly because he didn't want anyone to see the extent to which he had remodeled the place as a shrine to the dead Norman. According to Alden, this impulse to memorialize stemmed from love, pure and simple; only in cynical moments did Paul suspect his friend of trying to expiate a posthumous guilt. For since he'd been eighteen, Alden had had a habit of falling in love with eighteen-year-olds. The trouble was, everyone kept growing older — Norman kept getting older — while the world's supply of eighteen-year-olds remained inexhaustible.

No one had lied to Paul. Alden himself hadn't lied to him. Even before they'd slept together, he'd explained who Norman had been, come clean about his own HIV status, suggested, as if it were a business proposition, that if Paul might be willing to stick it out with him for a couple of years, a fairly large inheritance would be his reward. All of which, at first, had horrified Paul's innate and youthful sense of optimism. And yet in a world where people ran away without saying good-bye, perhaps business arrangements, in the end, were more trustworthy than love affairs. So he had accepted Alden's terms, and to his surprise, discovered that he felt more than he would have expected. Not love, exactly; instead something more serene and reliable than love: fondness alloyed with esteem.

"By the way, I had a real surprise coming home this afternoon," Paul said. "I ran into someone I knew in the elevator."

"Oh? Who was that?"

"Joseph Mansourian. He said he knew you too."

"Oh, sure. He's up on the twenty-third floor. Where did you meet him?"

"San Francisco."

"It's probably a good thing you ran into him," Alden said. "He could help you. No one has more influence in the piano world than Mansourian." Then he went into his study to make some some phone calls. Sitting down at the piano, Paul played, rather absentmindedly, the first few bars of a Chopin étude. The truth was, he was still trying to assess his own feelings about the encounter with Mr. Mansourian. Relief was certainly in the forefront; what had tormented Paul most in the months after Rome hadn't been so much Kennington's abandonment itself as its lack of explanation. And the ground that silence left barren, speculation filled in. Perhaps there'd been an emergency. Perhaps a message had been left, and lost. Or perhaps Pamela had scared him off with her loud neediness, or Paul himself, by making some faux pas, the severity of which he'd been too naive to recognize: the social equivalent of turning two pages at once. For months he'd known nothing. Now, however, he knew at least that Kennington hadn't said anything about the affair to Mr. Mansourian, for which he was glad. If he had, Paul would have recognized it instantly in Mansourian's eyes.

A toilet flushed. Buttoning up his pants, Alden returned. "So what do you feel like having for dinner? Chinese?"

"Fine," Paul said, suddenly abandoning Chopin in favor of a Scarlatti sonata. Meanwhile Alden took the stack of take-out menus out of the bureau drawer. "How does chicken with mustard greens sound to you?"

"Fine."

"And cold noodles with sesame sauce, of course —"

"Alden." Paul lifted his fingers from the keys. "This Mansourian, does he have a boyfriend?"

"I don't know. Probably."

"I only wondered because when I met him in San Francisco, I had the distinct feeling he was coming on to me."

"I'm sure he was."

"So he must be single."

"Ha!" Alden picked up the phone to dial. "You know the saying. When the cat's away, the mouse will play."

"Yes, but —"

"Not that the cat *has* to be away. The cat merely has to be at the office, or out shopping, or — hello, Empire Szechwan? Yes, I can. Why, even as we speak I suspect Joseph Mansourian is sitting upstairs in his boudoir, plotting how to get into your pants."

"No he isn't!"

"It makes me think how lucky I am that I got to you first." He scratched Paul's head. "Because if you ask me . . . hello? Yes, this is Alden Haynes calling. How are you this evening? I was wondering if I might order some food to be delivered . . ."

The next morning Paul woke up so early that he was showered and on his way to school even before Alden's alarm had gone off. Out the revolving doors he hurried, his eyes peeled for Mansourian, whom he didn't see. Breath formed cartoon speech bubbles before his eyes as he trudged uptown, glancing now and then at the tangles of Christmas bulbs that spanned Broadway, somewhat forlorn in their switched-off state, in the greasy gray winter light. They reminded him that in just a couple of weeks he was going to have to fly home, to face his mother for the first time since summer: his mother, who had written him a letter at 4:12 A.M. Needless to say she knew nothing of his New York life, nor was he inclined to tell her.

In a deli just across the street from Juilliard, he ordered coffee and a buttered bagel, of which he was just taking his first bite when Jen Feeney, a girl of indiscriminate friendliness, accosted him. "Hey, Paul!" she said, stabbing at the plastic top of her coffee cup. "Say, have you heard the news?"

"What news?"

"Thang Po's been signed on by Joseph Mansourian. You know, the kid who's giving the recital this afternoon."

Paul swayed on his heels. Of course he knew Thang, who at fourteen was the youngest student in their class. He'd just never bothered to take him seriously.

"But how did it happen?"

"Well, it's really an inspiring story. I mean, Thang was a boat person. His parents had nothing. *Nothing.* They run a grocery in Queens, if you can believe it! Then apparently on Kirchenwald's recommendation he played for Joseph Mansourian last week and the guy signed him on just like that."

She snapped her fingers. "*The* Joseph Mansourian. Can you imagine?"

Paul could. Indeed, as he walked (or rather, limped) across Broadway, pangs of grief assailed him. Why hadn't Kirchenwald asked *him* to play for Mr. Mansourian? After all, he liked Paul; just last week had praised his Schumann. And yet could he have really thought Paul that good if he had favored Thang, and not him, with such a introduction?

They arrived at school. "So will I see you at the recital this afternoon?" Jen asked. "Personally, I can't wait."

"I guess," Paul answered. In fact, ever since the deli he'd been trying to figure out how to escape the recital, since Thang's newfound success had had the effect of throwing his own comparative obscurity into relief. Still, better the devil you knew than the devil you didn't; his mother always said that. So he went. In the auditorium he sat between Jen and an extremely tall girl from Scarsdale who wore pearls and was called Oona Ford.

Oona Ford had also heard the news. "My, the Schumann fantasy," she said, scanning her program. "That second movement's a pianistic waterloo if there ever was one. If he's not careful," she added in a low voice, "Thang Po may end up being a very *po' thang* indeed."

"Oona!" Jen laughed. "That's a terrible joke. And racist!" A rebuke to which Oona responded by raising her hands into the air.

"Far be it from me to voice an unpopular opinion, but you know as well as I do that these little Asian prodigies — I

mean, yes, they can manage a certain technical proficiency —
but they play like robots! They're *soulless*."

"Oona, I can't believe what you're saying! How can you
generalize like that?"

"Name me one great Asian pianist."

"Asia is a huge continent. You can't lump together people
from Japan and China and Vietnam and —"

"I said, name me one great Asian pianist."

"That's not the point! And anyway, since when has virtuos-
ity been the opposite of feeling? I'm so tired of that old line!
You have to be technically proficient *before* you can —"

The lights dimmed. Onto the little stage the subject of the
argument now stepped. Aside from simple adjectives of race,
size, and age, he could not be described. Not merely diffident,
Thang was as close to abstract as any human being Paul had
ever seen. Nor did his clothes — white shirt and black pants,
like piano keys — improve matters. Instead they made him
look as if the instrument had consumed his personality, trans-
forming him into an anthropomorphic projection of its
mechanism.

Bowing listlessly, he sat. ("Now that's what I call a soulful
guy," Oona whispered.) His arms hung limp, like a rag doll's.
Yet when he started to play he grabbed Paul's attention so
forcefully it hurt.

Later, Paul would recall what Miss Novotna had once said
about Kennington — *it was as if Chopin were waiting for this
young man to be born*. For you couldn't be envious of playing
like that. It razored straight through rivalrous impulses to

quicken the very nerves and fibers of the body. It vouchsafed no reaction save joy.

"God, wasn't that incredible?" Jen said once the recital had ended. "I mean, have you ever heard anything like that?"

Oona, her face discomposed, snorted, then lit a cigarette.

"You know who he reminds me of more than anyone? You know who? He reminds me of Richard Kennington."

"Well, I've got to be going." Oona put on her coat and left. And shortly thereafter Jen, perhaps recognizing she'd talked too much, left too. Paul was now alone.

Just as he was pulling on his mittens, Thang emerged from the little door at the side of the stage. He was carrying a battered black briefcase. To Paul's surprise, no one accompanied him.

"Hi," Paul said, standing as he neared. "I'm Paul Porterfield. I'm in your class."

"Hi." The hand Thang held out was damp.

"I just wanted to say that was really an incredible concert. I mean, maybe one of the best performances of the fantasy I've ever heard. Congratulations."

"Thanks. I dropped a note in the march, though."

"Really? I didn't notice."

"Uh-huh."

"Well, I wouldn't worry about it too much. The audience loved you. Obviously."

"I guess." Thang shifted from one foot to the other. For a few awkward seconds, two boys, they just stood there.

"Well, I've got to go," Thang said eventually. "My mother's picking me up."

"Okay. Nice to meet you."

"Nice to meet you too."

Thang disappeared. Through the half-open door Paul saw a woman's face, weathered, in wait.

Afterward, walking along Broadway toward Alden's apartment, he tried to sort out his reaction to the recital. Jealousy, he could not deny it, was an ingredient, though not the primary one. Perhaps it was more accurate to say that the performance compelled him to examine and to some extent rework his definition of genius. Questions fired in Paul. What was it about Thang's playing? Was Paul, as a pianist, in the same league? With Kennington it had been different: Kennington had been an abstraction when Paul had first encountered him, a disembodied series of tones coming through his childhood record player. Whereas Thang was a peer. A colleague.

He stopped for a red light. Something crucial happened. He answered his own question. The answer was no.

He blinked. Above him the Christmas lights flashed alive. Stars and bells, frosty with glitter, haloed pockets of cold air.

"I shall never be what I hoped," he said next, as if trying on the words for fit. "Thang Po, yes. Paul Porterfield . . ." But he couldn't finish his sentence.

How odd! From those ethereally remote days of four months ago (he heard it "as if from a distance," like one of the indications for Schumann's *Davidsbündlertänze*) some music sounded: it was *Peter and the Wolf,* a jaunty melody of seeking into the very logic of which was woven the assurance of a happy end. *And to think* (Paul thought) *that once I trotted down hallways with that in my head, the accompaniment to how I was sure my life was going to go.* Yet it was the music of innocence, clear and bright and spacious. And now it was finished. Now it was done. For Thang had surprised Paul into the saddest revelation of his life. That was his gift. His playing bypassed ambition to percuss a deeper chord, a more loving chord, a chord that yanked Paul to his feet, pulled his hands (also Oona's) one against the other to make, in response to that sacred noise, a brutish, even bestial noise — like seals barking, Paul had always thought. And they were seals barking. That was why Oona had looked so discomposed. It ruffled her to see her cultivations so rudely stripped away, to be rendered as mute as the animals Orpheus charmed, wagging their languageless tongues for more.

*Never mine,* a voice inside him said, *the pleasure of gathering the animals.*

He was back now. At Alden's building. From where he guarded the revolving door, the young doorman winked. And did he have a dark cock with a long foreskin, that doorman? (On his finger a gold wedding band, patinaed.)

Paul got in the elevator (he sat), rode to the sixteenth floor (he stood), undid the double doors with their double locks. He smelled cooking, heard music . . . but where was it coming from?

Moving cautiously down the hall, he peered through the half-open door to the living room. Apparently the cleaning lady, who was forgetful, had left the television on. An elderly cartoon was playing. Flowers with baby faces opened their petals, robins chirruped and darted, all to the tune of Mendelssohn.

Very quietly he took off his coat, slipped off his shoes, lay down on the floor.

He watched. The music changed. In the cartoon a fox appeared. The flowers zipped up their petals like parkas. The birds took to the trees.

Then the fox pounced.

A ringing sounded. At first Paul thought it was part of the cartoon, until he realized that it was the telephone, and picked it up.

"Hello?"

"Alden?"

"No, Paul."

"Paul, Joseph Mansourian here! How are you?"

"Fine, fine." Sitting up, Paul muted the television, brushed back his hair.

"I hope you don't mind my calling you at Alden's."

"It's okay."

"Good. You see, aside from needing an excuse to tell you what a pleasure it was running into you in the elevator yesterday, I wanted to let you know that I was talking to Louis Kirchenwald this morning, and your name came up."

"It did?"

"Yes. I don't know if you've heard, but I've just signed on a classmate of yours, Thang Po."

"Yes, I heard. I was at his recital today."

"Amazing, isn't he? I owe Louis a favor for that. So anyway, as I was saying, he and I were chatting this morning, and I happened to inquire if he could give me the name of a student I might ask —"

"Oh, Mr. Mansourian —"

"About page turning."

"Page turning?"

"Yes. You see, on Friday Thang's going to play some chamber music with a few friends here at my apartment. Just a little private get-together. Thang and Tushi Strauss are doing the *Kreutzer,* after which Thang's playing a Liszt group. It'll be quite casual, bear in mind, just twenty people or so. Kennington may even be there, if he gets back from Tokyo in time."

"Really."

"So can you do it?"

"Sure . . . I mean, thank you."

"Oh, good. I'm delighted. Well, you know where I live. It's the twenty-third floor. Why don't you come by around six on Friday?"

"That'll be great."

"See you soon, then."

"Bye."

They hung up. For a moment, having replaced the telephone receiver in its cradle, Paul stared at the muted television. Then he brought the sound back up and lay down again on his stomach. Another cartoon had started. Tom and Jerry. A lion, it seemed, had escaped from the zoo and was hiding in the basement of that huge, humanless house in which cat and mouse, perpetually, tormented each other.

In such a posture Alden discovered him, when he came home from work half an hour later. Paul's face on the floor, and the carpet wet with tears.

"Paul, what's wrong?" he asked.

"Never mine," Paul answered.

"Never mind?"

"Never mind." And he cried like a baby.

# 13

ONCE AGAIN, Paul was the page turner. At Joseph's piano, he sat to the left of Thang, eyes on the score, which he handled flawlessly. Kirchenwald was there, looking proud, as were Thang's parents; Izzy Gerstler (he didn't seem to recognize Paul); even Oona, who to Paul's mild surprise had arrived with Thang himself. As for Kennington, he never showed up, having apparently decided to stop off a few days in Kyoto before flying home.

A reception followed the recital. In the living room the assembled guests grouped themselves naturally into little aggregates of four and five, while white-gloved waiters moved in and out of the swinging kitchen door, bearing shrimp and canapés and glasses of cold white wine on silver trays. Only Paul had no one to talk to. Instead, feeling rather conspicuous in his dark suit, he looked at the photographs on the walls and bookshelves, many of which featured Kennington. In one he was a boy, shaking hands with Richard Nixon. In another he was sharing an ice cream cone with a dachshund. In a third he was a young man, throwing a coin into the Trevi Fountain. Then there were the photographs of Kennington *with* Mansourian, who from what Paul could see had been handsome as a younger man. In various concert halls, against arrangements of flowers and pianos, they smiled forth, foreheads shiny. Or they lay side by side on a beach, Kennington lean and boyish in a blue-checked bathing suit. (The dachshund was in this one too.) Or Kennington sat at the very piano where Thang had just played, holding an argyle sweater up to his chest, a Christmas tree winking behind him.

Soon a voice interrupted this reverie. "Hello, Paul," Joseph said. "Enjoying my little gallery?"

"Yes, I am. And so many of Mr. Kennington!"

"He and I go back a lot of years." A waiter neared with a trayful of wineglasses, one of which Joseph handed to Paul. "Let's drink a toast, then. To our well-dressed page turner."

The glasses crashed. "By the way," Paul added, pointing to the picture of the Trevi Fountain, "this photograph — when was it taken?"

"That one?" Joseph put on his reading glasses. "Oh yes. As you can see, Richard was doing his Jean Peters imitation."

"Jean Peters?"

"Haven't you seen *Three Coins in a Fountain*? Really, Paul, you'll lose your card for that."

"My card —"

"As for when it was taken" — Joseph held the picture at a distance — "some time in the late seventies, judging from the lapels." He smiled. "I must get back to Rome. I used to go with Richard all the time. But then it was so hard to travel, on account of my dog. She died this summer."

"Oh, I'm sorry."

"Thank you." Joseph took a sip of wine. "Most people, they think the death of a dog doesn't mean much. But Sophie was like a child to me."

"Have you thought of getting another dog?"

"Oh, I couldn't. Not yet. You have to respect the grieving process, it seems to me. On the other hand, some people think that as soon as one thing's over, the best thing to do is move on to another. But here I go, off on a sidetrack, when what we were talking about was dogs."

Looking away from the photographs, toward the little nucleus of attention that had formed around Thang, Paul said, "It's true, what you said about grieving. For instance, I know someone whose friend died, and the first thing he did was go out and look for a replacement."

"They're afraid of being alone. Terrified of being alone." Joseph edged nearer. "By the way, do you have any plans for dinner tonight?"

"No."

"Why don't you stay, then? I'll order something in."

Paul looked Joseph steadily in the eye for a moment. "Sure," he said.

"Wonderful, wonderful. Well, listen, I'd better be getting back to my hostly duties. After all, good-bye is the most important part of the job, they say. You'll excuse me, won't you? And in the meantime feel free to do whatever you need to keep yourself, you know, amused."

"Oh, I've always been good at amusing myself."

"Good. Well, till later." And he headed off to say his professional farewells: first to Tushi and her young man, then to Kirchenwald, then to Thang's parents. As for Thang himself, he and Oona Ford were on the couch now, engaged in a surprisingly intimate tête-à-tête.

Soon they left as well. Paul, sensing that he ought to keep a low profile, had by this time ensconced himself in the alcove with the CD and record collection, where he was looking at another photograph. It was one of those contract-signing shots that are such a staple of the classical music world. In it Kennington, still boyish, stood with a pen poised over the sheets, while men in dark suits watched him hungrily.

After a moment, Joseph joined him. "Alone at last," he said.

"I was just looking at your records," Paul said. "I've never seen such a big collection."

"Goes with the job." Joseph loosened his tie. "So what would you like to drink, Paul?"

"Nothing, thanks. By the way, I couldn't help but notice how many recordings you've got of Mahler's Fifth."

"A particular favorite of mine."

"Oh, and here's *Richter in Italy!*" Paul pulled an old LP from the shelf. "I've been looking for that for years. Wow, it's even autographed."

"Take it."

"No, no. I didn't mean —"

"Go on, take it," Joseph repeated, pressing the record into Paul's hands. "I never listen to it anyway."

"Really? Thank you."

They were quiet for a few seconds, their eyes on the spines of the CDs. Soon Paul felt a tingling on his scalp that gradually deepened into a caress.

"You have nice hair," Joseph said, pressing his fingers into Paul's temples.

"Mmm."

"You sure you're not thirsty?"

"I'm fine."

"Say, I know. How would you like to hear a tape of Richard's new Chopin recording? Harry Moore gave me an advance copy."

"I'd love to."

Removing his hand from Paul's head, Joseph extracted a cassette from one of the drawers below the CD shelves. "You're going to be one of the first people in the world to hear this," he said, inserting the cassette into the stereo.

The music began. "The *Barcarolle,*" Paul said distantly.

Again Joseph ran his fingers through Paul's hair.

Paul closed his eyes. Joseph turned him around and kissed him.

"What are you doing tomorrow night?" he asked when the kiss was over.

"Nothing."

"Would you like to hear the Berlin Philharmonic?"

"But it's sold out."

"I have tickets."

"I'd love to, if you're sure it won't be a problem."

"Of course it won't be a problem. We'll make an evening of it, how about that? First drinks here, then dinner at Café Luxembourg, then the concert."

"Sounds great."

Moving back into the living room, Joseph sat down on the sofa. "Come sit by me," he said, patting the spot to his left.

Paul sat. Almost immediately Joseph's arm went around his shoulders.

For the second time, they kissed.

After a minute Paul pulled away. "I'm sorry, but would you mind changing the music?"

"Sure."

"It's not that I don't like it . . . it's just —"

"You don't have to explain," Joseph said, bouncing up and removing the cassette from the stereo. "Just tell me what you'd like to hear instead."

"Anything. Scarlatti."

"Scarlatti, Scarlatti . . ." With his fingernail he scanned the CDs. "Ah, here we are. And whose Scarlatti would you prefer? I've got Horowitz, Landowska, Pletnev, Pogorelich, Charles Rosen on the Siena Pianoforte, Schiff, Maria Tipo, Alexis Weissenberg, Christian Zacharias —"

"Horowitz."

"Horowitz it is." Pulling the gem case from the shelf, Joseph removed the CD and laid it carefully on its bed. Then he returned to the sofa.

"Is that better?" he asked.

"Yes. That's good."

Again, they kissed. The fingers of Joseph's right hand made circles over Paul's chest; slipped between the buttons of his shirt.

"You've got a very nice musculature," he said.

"Thank you."

"Let me see what you look like."

Obediently Paul stood. He undid his tie. *And so it has come to this,* he found himself thinking as he unbuttoned, *the way it might have begun, in San Francisco* . . . yet he was not unhappy, nor unaroused. Instead, as he opened his belt, and peered over at Joseph, who was watching him urgently, he could feel the lust rising in his own throat. Also in his pants.

Eyes closed, he pulled his T-shirt over his head, sat again, his nipples hardening. He thought of Thang, his hands.

"You're a beautiful boy," Joseph said. He palmed Paul's chest like a blind man, while Horowitz played, and the pictures in their frames stared from the piano.

# 14

"PAUL, DEAR," Miss Novotna said, "it's called the *Well-tempered Clavier,* not the *Ill-tempered Clavier.*"

"I'm sorry," Paul said. "I'll start again."

"No, don't start again. Sit down over there. There, we shall have some tea. Consuelo! Tea! And some of those Peek Freans!"

Folding her hands in her lap, Miss Novotna smiled across the table at Paul, who was fidgeting in his chair. It was just past noon on Christmas Eve, and he was visiting his old teacher for the first time since starting Juilliard. She kept her apartment dark these days, he noticed. Heavy curtains, drawn to meet, blockaded the winter sunlight, a few rays of which nonetheless broke through to illuminate a bust of Kessler here, a photograph of Kessler there, the Mason and Hamlin piano, from which dust particles rose, only to resettle on other, older, dustier things.

"You are not playing your best today," Miss Novotna said, adjusting one of her rings.

He looked away. "Not an easy Christmas. My parents are divorcing."

"Oh, I'm sorry."

"Thank you. My mother's very depressed."

"And how is school?"

Paul cracked his knuckles.

"Don't do that, it brings on arthritis. Now how is school?"

"School is . . . all right. Not great."

"And Kirchenwald?"

"Fine. He's not like you, of course. Also : . . I don't know. He just doesn't seem very *interested* in me." Paul rested his cheek on his fist. "To be honest, he's much more interested in a boy called Thang Po. Have you heard of him? Joseph Mansourian's already signed him on. He's going to Brussels for the Queen Elisabeth."

"Ah, the Queen Elisabeth."

"Yes. And I'm jealous. At least I admit it. No one else will. I'm not going to Brussels, though. I don't think I'm ready."

"Judging from your performance today, Paul, I'm afraid I must agree."

He glanced up, startled a little bit not to be contradicted.

"I have to be honest," she continued. "You have fallen off since the summer. What I had hoped Juilliard would develop in you . . . that quality of sincerity, of holding the music together . . . I do not hear. No, don't interrupt!" She stood and hobbled over to the old record player. "I am going to play you something. I am going to play you the adagio of the *Hammerklavier.* Listen."

Then she sat down again, and they listened. It is a difficult adagio, one that only a great pianist can keep from falling apart. And in these hands it did not fall apart; it was more than broken things, even though broken things were what it spoke of. Paul heard a voice that was tired, perhaps of life. Then a cuckoo seemed to call slowly, softly — not like a cuckoo at all. And the voice sustained the ability to go on. Nothing so poetic as peace, or a reconciliation . . . just that stark sentence: the voice sustained the ability to go on.

When it was over, Miss Novotna lifted the needle from the record with a shaky hand. "It is very sad," Paul said, as she passed him a box of tissues.

"Yes, it is."

After a moment, he said, "I shall never play like that, shall I?"

His teacher stared for a few seconds at the tabletop. "No," she answered at length. "No, I suspect you will not."

"And yet earlier you seemed to think—"

"That was my failure. It is possible to see one thing one moment, and then later realize —"

"But Miss Novotna, if I can't be a pianist, what am I going to do? I'm not good at anything else."

"Nonsense. You can do anything you wish. Go to medical school, or law school. Or write. That is, if you can't bear remaining in the world of music. If that's the case, I understand. It is easier, perhaps, for women, to take a supporting role, to become teachers and nurturers, accompanists —"

"Page turners," Paul interrupted.

"To be a page turner is not a profession," Miss Novotna said quickly. "To be an accompanist, on the other hand, is a noble calling. You might consider that option. Certainly you could make a success of it, since as I've always said —"

"Will carries an artist further than talent. I know."

"Precisely. And will, Paul, you possess in abundance."

"But talent only enough to accompany brilliant violinists and cellists and singers, is that what you're saying?"

"I'm only trying to spare you future suffering," Miss Novotna answered stiffly. "Believe me, if you prove me wrong and become one of the great pianists of your day, I shall be the first to admit my misjudgment. But if you do not, and this is likely for anyone, then it's best to decide now whether you can bear accepting a secondary role."

"The way you did."

She bowed her head.

"And yet it seems so unfair! When Kennington was my age, he'd already —"

"Do not speak of him like that!" Miss Novotna lifted her hand peremptorily. "Remember, this is a man who lives for music itself. Keep that in your mind when you speak of him. Otherwise he becomes for you nothing more than a projection of your own ambition. And Kennington has never been concerned with ambition. To him fame is a grief. It is what gets in the way."

"Oh, what I wouldn't give to worry about fame getting in the way!"

"Don't have any illusions about pain," Miss Novotna said. "You are still a child in this regard. A child believes that joy is infinite and suffering is short. And why shouldn't he believe that? He scrapes his knee, it heals. Another child is cruel, he cries. Yet his mother always loves him. And then he grows up, and his mother dies, and he learns that the opposite of everything he believed is true. Joy is short, but suffering . . . suffering lasts."

"Miss Novotna —"

She raised her hand. "And now," she said, "I must see what is keeping Consuelo with that tea."

Lifting herself creakily out of her chair, she left. In the dark, dusty room, the swimming bars of light defined a border that Paul now crossed more easily than he could have imagined possible. He picked up the jacket of the record Miss Novotna had just played for him, and saw on the cover her own young face.

# 15

CHRISTMAS WAS OVER. It had passed, as usual, in a fever of generosities, and left an aftertaste of swindle in its wake. Nothing had gone as Paul's mother had hoped, by which she meant that the turkey was dry; she had bought Paul the wrong recording of the Rachmaninoff Third; the volume knob had broken off George's new Walkman. On top of which one of the P's had disappeared from the Scrabble set. "Anticippointment," Pamela said, feeding the wrapping paper to the flames, and there was in that invented word all the regret and resignation that forty-seven years of Christmases had built up in her. For despite what she had been promised since infancy, suffering and worry had not taken the day off. Pain had not taken the day off. A rent breached the universe, one that neither comfort nor joy could heal. Nor would the *Hammerklavier* have taught her anything she didn't already know. She understands the drill. When life can only be borne a minute at a time, you measure out your life in minutes. Then the hours make themselves. The days make themselves. And you sustain the ability to go on.

Why was she so sorrowful? She had not loved her husband. Still, his presence was something to which she had become habituated. And now he would have nothing to do with her, and when she woke on Christmas morning, it was to face the uncomfortable image of a woman ragged at the edges, fingernails dirty, the dye growing out of her hair. He did not love her: that was the painful part. And Kennington did not love her either; she had taken a misunderstanding for a miracle; she had let the chasm of hope yawn open, had leapt over it from sorrow into joy, a journey that is perhaps always better taken slowly, the long way round. Now, ensconced in sorrow's hinterlands, she looked out at the scarred patch of earth where hope had closed, and vowed never to be fooled again. She never was. Perhaps to be loved one must always run the risk of being fooled. In any case, what happiness she knew in later years, and it was ample, would be entirely of her own making.

Sorrow is perhaps the most selfish of emotions. Certainly it is the most voracious. It eats up the food of the spirit, and empathy starves. Therefore it will probably come as little surprise that Pamela failed to register her son's suffering that Christmas. Instead, when she looked at him, and at George and his wife, Christine (her daughter, Julie, was with her in-laws), she saw only youth, which insults age with its heedless insouciance. How could he not rejoice, she asked herself, having every chance for joy ahead of him? Yet he was glum. His brother and sister-in-law noticed it too. At breakfast with their father he spoke ill of their mother. Then at dinner with their mother he spoke ill of their father. He seemed without loyalties, when in fact his aggression was merely affixing itself to any stray target that came its way. For it seemed that no sooner would he start coming to grips with Miss Novotna's sad assessments, than someone would be thrusting a piano-key scarf in his face. Every present that year was music: in his stocking gold-plated cuff links shaped like tiny pianos, new CDs, books about romanticism, and blue Henle scores. And his brother wanted him to play. "Schumann!" George demanded, but Paul, remembering Thang, shook his head.

"Then how about Prokofiev? Play *Peter and the Wolf.*" George was sitting with Christine on the sofa, fashioning a new P for the Scrabble set from a piece of plywood.

"It's not written for the piano, although there is a transcription by Tatiana Nikolayeva."

Instead he played "Romeo Bids Juliet Farewell" — badly. His brother and sister-in-law got distracted and started talking about how much they'd loved *Peter and the Wolf* as children. "And wasn't the duck the clarinet?" (The cat was the clarinet.)

"When we have our five children —"

"Our three children —"

"When we have our five children —"

So the holy day proceeded, and in the end, perhaps the best that can be said for it, at least so far as the Porterfields were concerned, is that it was gotten through. When midnight struck at last, the tides of the future immersed that island of Christmas over which the world, for a few weeks, had fussed and doted. And in the resulting ocean, Paul saw Kennington. Was he drowning? He hoped not. In New York, in addition to Alden, with whom he had continued more or less to live,

Paul had started having an affair with Joseph Mansourian, whom he had once found so unattractive, and from whom he had learned, among other things, that Kennington was in town again. Also from Joseph — or more specifically, from Joseph's Rolodex — he had gotten Kennington's address and phone number. He'd called several times, never leaving messages; even spent an afternoon standing across the street from the building on White Street where Kennington lived. But when, around four-thirty, Kennington finally emerged, he'd had to hide. The sight of his erstwhile lover after so many months, handsome and windblown, stunned him into a peculiar reluctance, a hesitancy to approach. For if he loved this man (and he was sure he did), then why was he sleeping with Alden? Why was he sleeping with Joseph? Well, the answer was obvious: it was because this man did not love him, and in the meantime he had to get on in the world, didn't he? He had to forget. And yet how could he forget, when Kennington's face was everywhere in Joseph's apartment, so omnipresent that Paul couldn't seem to turn around without confronting it? With that face, in all the stages of its growth, he had regained, over the weeks, an intimacy, so much so that when the time came to fly home for Christmas he could hardly bear to part with it. Which was why, in Menlo Park, the photograph of his friend throwing a coin into the Trevi Fountain lay buried amid the carefully folded T-shirts in Paul's suitcase. His last afternoon he'd swiped it from the bookcase, taken it back to his apartment, removed it carefully from its frame. On the back someone — Joseph or Kennington — had written, "You are all that I wish for"; yet even in fantasy, Paul could never quite convince himself that the message was meant for him.

The next morning he and his mother woke early and drove to Walgreen's to shop for Christmas cards and wrapping paper. Beginning on the twenty-sixth, Christmas cards and wrapping paper were half price, and Pamela liked to buy up a supply in advance, so that the following year she could congratulate herself on her economy.

Together, as was their ritual, they pushed the cart down the aisle. They did not speak. Too much family activity had diluted that intimacy that had evolved between them in the years after George and Julie went off to school. Only now, in this drugstore where they had spent so many hours, did a certain desultory humor return to them, a humor cultivated over years of being left alone together at the end of holidays. Wheels squeaked. Pamela threw bags of colored bows and bright cylinders of paper into the cart (their value slashed, they glimmered with pathos) while Paul kept an eye out for the video camera in the corner. As a boy he'd made a game of running to the cash register just as his mother passed so that he could see her face captured in the closed-circuit television. Now, of course, a more brooding eye peered down, watchful for darker thefts.

Pamela wanted to know how school was going. Because Paul's decision to commit himself to the piano had more or less coincided with Kelso's (unannounced) defection, not to

mention the departure of his brother and sister for midwest-
ern cities, only his mother had really shared in its evolution.
Now she asked the questions he had hoped to be spared: Was
Juilliard a success? Were his teachers a success? Did they
recognize the jewel they held in their hands?

"I'm thinking of quitting" was Paul's answer.

"What?" Pamela stopped the cart.

"I'm just not so sure the performing life is really for me.
Maybe I'd do better, I don't know, working for a music agent,
or writing liner notes. Or going to law school."

"Now, Paul, wait a minute. I'm sorry, but I can't quite
believe what I'm hearing. You want to quit the piano?"

"Why not?"

"But you love the piano!"

"So?"

"And anyway, you're so good! Everyone says so. Mr. Wang,
Miss Novotna —"

"Not anymore. We talked about it the day before yesterday,
and she agrees with me."

"Agrees with you! She must be senile!"

"She's not senile in the least."

Opening her purse, Pamela pulled out a tissue. "I'm sorry,"
she said again, rubbing her nose. "I'm just shocked. I can't
imagine what's gotten into you."

"Maybe the truth . . . that I'm not good enough."

"But I've heard you, and I think —"

"You only think I'm good because I'm your son. You know

nothing about music. Now please, can we change the sub-
ject?"

They stumbled to the cash register. With supreme effort,
Pamela pulled herself together enough to pay and make small
talk with the cashier; only once they were safe in the car did
she start to weep. And of course she was weeping not only for
Paul's failures: she was weeping for her husband, whom she
had failed to love, and for Kennington, who had failed to love
her; and for a failed French exam; and a hundred private
failures, with which this story is not concerned.

Meanwhile Paul sat in his place, bristly with impatience,
until his mother blew her nose again and turned the key in the
ignition.

"Okay, come out with it," he said. "You might as well tell
me what's on your mind."

"There's nothing on my mind. I think it's too early, that's
all." (They were pulling out of the parking lot.) "I mean, why
not finish out the year at least, honey? You may feel differ-
ently then."

"I think I can fairly assume —"

"Assume makes an ass of you and me. And anyway, once
you quit —"

"I'm not going to end up on skid row, if that's what you're
worried about. I'll do fine. Get a job or something, like a
normal person."

"But you're not —" She bit her lip.

"What? I'm not what?"

"Paul, I'm sorry, I have to say it. I can't help but wonder if that man —"

"What man?"

"If *he* had something to do with this."

"Who? Kennington?"

She nodded. "I know we haven't talked about it since he ran out on us. And I haven't mentioned it to your brother and sister, either. None of it."

"Neither have I."

"Still, you can't blame me for putting two and two together. I know he made quite an impression on you. And so when you start talking like this I can't help but think that he might have . . . I don't know, made you lose your confidence, somehow, honey. Will you move? The goddamned light is green!"

"You're wrong."

"What did you talk about, all those afternoons?"

"Nothing. Music, art. Life."

"Have you seen him since you've been in New York?"

"No."

"I'm sure he must have said something to you in Rome. Something you're not telling me. Oh, if I could get my hands on that man, I'd wring his neck!"

"Mother, for the last time, he has nothing to do with it. Now will you please calm down? I didn't confide in you so that you could become completely hysterical, I confided in you because I needed some advice — a mistake, since obviously I could get more reasoned advice from a cat than from you."

"Paul, don't talk to me like that!"

"So from now on, when I need advice, I'll go elsewhere, all right? Oh, for God's sake, don't cry!"

"I can't help it."

"Mother, we are in the middle of traffic! We are in the middle of a fucking intersection!"

"It's just been such an awful Christmas —"

"Pull over. I'll drive."

She did. He drove.

By the time they got home she had steadied herself.

"Paul, honey," she said, as they carried the bags to the kitchen, "I want to say one thing —"

"No more. Otherwise I leave. Now."

She stopped talking. George and Christine announced that they were going to the shopping center, and Paul decided to accompany them: he wanted to exchange the wrong Rachmaninoff Third for the right one.

The car crunched gravel under its wheels, and Pamela was alone.

In the sudden silence, she vacuumed. Blue towel dust, bits of bread crumb and eggshell, disappeared obediently up the tube. Then a penny got stuck in the bag, making a racket like a pinball machine. She moved on to Paul's room, where she vacuumed patterns in the nap of the carpet, blue and navy blue. For it was her duty to save him, and when she could not fulfill her duty, her energy went into housework. She did housework all the time these days. The house glowed with the burnt cleanliness of an obsessively washed hand.

It was when she thrust the nozzle under the bed that

it encountered the obstruction. A sock or some underwear, Pamela thought, and was surprised, when she reached under, to pull out a magazine. And how funny! Santa Claus was on the cover — but a young Santa Claus, his jacket unbuttoned, his chest bared. And inside the magazine, Santa Claus again, wearing only his fur-lined red pants! But why . . .

She flipped the page and screamed. The vacuum cleaner, abandoned, whined as if with hunger. Her hands shaking, she picked the magazine up from where it had fallen.

"Santa's got a special present for you," the text read. "He's not coming down the chimney this year!"

Closing the magazine, she stuffed it back under the bed, and resumed her vacuuming.

# 16

PAMELA WASN'T SURE whether to make the sour cream coffee cake or the lemon nut bars. Generally speaking the sour cream coffee cake was more of a crowd pleaser; then again the lemon nut bars were her own recipe. Finally she decided to make both (it took her the better part of three hours), after which, evading the Christmas tree, which had started shedding its needles, she went to examine herself in the mirror. Her hair, dyed in Rome, was gradually being reclaimed by its natural gray-blond tones, as if by some voracious species of weed. And how thin she looked! A sack of hot bones in a scratchy sweater, pilled and pulled, the frayed sleeves stretching so far below her hands that she could clutch at the hems, was even now clutching at the hems, with bitten fingernails.

"All right," she said, "enough," and pulled the sweater over her head. "Enough," she repeated, running a brush through her hair; though it was too late to get it cut, at least she could untangle some of the knots. Next she put on the pretty pink outfit she'd bought at Valentino, spritzed some perfume onto her neck, gathered up the desserts, and headed into the garage. Ten to seven in the evening on the fifth of January: the kids gone almost a week. "I must take that thing down," she

reminded herself as she passed the drooping tree, still fes-
tooned with ornaments they had made in their childhood.
Still, she could not quite bear the idea, not because she felt any
sentimental attachment to the thing, but because the prospect
of denuding it spoke too much to her of endings. Her stomach
clenched at the image of the corpse lying next to the garbage
cans, a few strands of tinsel still clinging to its branches, as if
to say, This is what it comes down to: we make an adored icon
of a thing, only to hurl it out to languish in bad weather. And
when we pass it every day, the filaments of tinsel, gleaming in
the winter sunlight, seem almost to wink at us: all hope mur-
dered. *There is no greater woe than to recall past bliss in misery.*

In the car, she tried not to think about where she was going.
Indeed, only when she found herself turning left into Diane
Moss's cul-de-sac did the first surge of panic seize her; sud-
denly she could not go through with it, and circling swiftly
round the little eyelet at the end of the cul-de-sac — it always
reminded her of spermatozoa — headed toward home. Then,
halfway there, she changed her mind again, not because some
new bravery had announced itself in her, but because the
prospect of another evening alone, with only the dead Christ-
mas tree to cheer her, seemed intolerable. At least the meeting
was company. And so she made another U-turn, crawled
cautiously down the cul-de-sac, parked in front of the Mosses'
house. The driveway was already full of cars. Through the
living room windows she could see warm firelight, the glim-
mer of the Christmas tree, a big woman in red holding a mug
to her lips.

Cakes in hand, she rang the bell. "Pammy!" Diane said, kissing her on the cheek. "I'm so glad you came!"

"I brought these," she answered, handing Diane red boxes.

"Wonderful. I'll put them on the buffet. Come on in." Diane ushered her through into the living room, where eight or ten women, most of them Pamela's age or older, were hovering around the fireplace. Some talked; others kept to themselves. One glanced at her assessingly. Diane's dining room chairs were arranged to form a circle with the sofa and armchairs, while on the buffet an array of cakes and cookies had been spread out, so opulent it might have been a Christmas party. And what a weird, yet soothing, coincidence that when she had called the support group number, Diane had answered! She would have never guessed about Teddy. Also soothing to note that she was not the only one whom the meeting had inspired to bake.

Brushing crumbs off her skirt, which was tartan plaid and fastened with a safety pin, Diane strode to the center of the room. "All right, ladies," she said, sitting down on the sofa. "Shall we begin?"

The other women took their places.

"We have a few new members to our group whom I'd like to welcome. First, Enid." (She indicated the large woman in red.)

"Hello," Enid said.

"Hello," the others answered in unison.

Enid coughed, extracted a mint from her black pocketbook. "I'm not sure where to begin," she admitted.

"Just take your time. You're among friends."

"All right. Well, the reason I'm here is that this Christmas my boy, my Allen, came home and told us that he was, you know, gay. And I've just been . . . well, I'm really having a hard time adjusting to it. I mean, you know, it's not something I ever expected to happen." (The other women nodded; they knew.) "Allen's a normal boy and all, he's not effeminate or anything, and it seems to me, he's only twenty-one, it's a little early for him to be making a choice, you know? But he says it isn't a choice." (She mangled her purse strap.) "So that's why I'm here. To find out what I should say because every time I try to talk to him I really put my foot in it."

She closed her lips. "Thank you, Enid," the women responded chorally, after which Diane added, "Our next new member is Caroline."

"Caro*lyn*," a gaunt woman in a beige pantsuit interrupted.

"Sorry. Carolyn."

"Mind if I smoke?" Given the go-ahead, Carolyn lit up. "Okay, I'm in a little bit of a different situation from you, Enid, because my son came out to me five years ago. The whole acceptance thing, we're already through that. I can handle his being gay. What I can't handle" — she exhaled — "is his lifestyle. He's twenty-five and he's not doing anything. He lives up in San Francisco and he works in this shop that's called — I'm not kidding — Does Your Mother Know?" (The other women laughed.) "And the thing is, I read about AIDS and all, and I really worry, because he's not in a steady relationship, and as far as I can tell he spends most of his time at the leather bars. I try to talk to him about it, I try to tell him he should find himself some nice guy and settle down, and he shuts me up. He says it's none of my business. Is there an ashtray?" (Diane handed her one.) "So that's why I'm here. I'm wondering if anyone else has had the same experience."

"Thank you, Carolyn," Diane said. "We'll talk about this after our third new member has spoken. Our third new member is Pamela. I have to interject here that Pamela is an old pal of mine. Our boys went to high school together, and now they're roommates in New York."

"Hello, Pamela."

"Hello." As was her habit in moments of anxiety, she balled a tissue in her fist. "Well, first of all, thank you, Diane, for inviting me. I'm also in a little bit of a different situation than the others because my son . . . well, he hasn't actually *told* me he's, um, gay." She gulped. "In fact . . . but I'm ashamed to admit it."

"Go on," Diane urged quietly.

"All right. The only reason I found out was that when he was home for Christmas I was cleaning his room one day — he was at the mall with his brother — and I found a magazine. You know, only men. God, I'm so embarrassed!"

"I did the same thing," one of the women said.

"It's okay, honey," another said.

"Anyway, after that, I — well, I guess I just have to come out with it. I went through his suitcase." She closed her eyes. "And there was a picture . . . a picture of a man we met when we were on vacation in Italy this summer. The picture showed him when he was younger, but I recognized him plain as day. And on the back he'd written" — again, she gulped — "You are all that I wish for."

She pulled at her lips.

"Well, it all clicked then. What was really going on when we were in Rome, why he and Paul spent nearly all their time together. I should have known, but I didn't. Then just as I was putting the picture back Pauly came home, and I had to stuff everything into the suitcase, and I think I must have put the clothes back differently than he'd had them — Paul's very fastidious about these things — because at dinner he kept looking at me strangely. And of course I had to stay quiet. I had to pretend nothing was going on. That was the worst part." She paused, drank some water from a glass that Diane had handed her. "So, as you can imagine, I've been having a very hard time with this. If I tell him I went through his things he'll be furious. On the other hand I want to get him away from this man because I'm convinced he's influencing Paul negatively."

She stopped talking. From across the room one of the other women, tall, with long black hair, dressed in lime green, was gazing at her with peculiar urgency.

"If you want to know what I think, you've got to tell him," Carolyn said.

"Come clean. Admit what you did. He'll be mad at first, but he'll get over it."

"Then you can move on to the more important things, like making sure he's practicing safe sex."

"But how can we know?"

"By being absolutely frank. You just say, sweetheart, let's talk turkey. Are you taking precautions?"

"Especially if your son's a bottom. No matter what the studies say, I'm absolutely convinced, it's more dangerous if they're bottoms."

"Whether they're tops or bottoms," Diane said, "the most important thing is to educate them about condom use. The younger boys don't always know the facts. For instance, only to use water-based lubricants."

"Otherwise the condoms disintegrate."

"And what about oral sex? *Is* oral sex safe?"

"I'm not sure. Some say yes, some say no. Certainly it's worse if you've got cuts in your mouth."

"Oh God." Enid started weeping. "Oh God, I can't stand it anymore. And his father hit him on the face. On Christmas day. My mother crying. Why me? My sister, all her boys —"

Enid howled. The other women comforted her. In the wake of such visceral pain, Pamela's own question had been forgotten. Such outbursts, she had the feeling, they knew how to manage. And yet AIDS — that was a different matter. There was suddenly unease in the room, as if with its mention some tenuous balance had been thrown off.

Meanwhile the woman across the way, the one in green, kept staring at her, moving her lips silently. What message was she trying to send?

After about an hour the official part of the meeting ended. The women descended upon the sideboard, attacking the food with a ferocity they would never have shown in the presence of men. Some cakes languished, while others — Pamela's sour cream in particular — went in a second. And from its popularity she derived an obscure sense of pride. How unlikely that at such a moment some vestige of old, ordinary experience, such as pride in baking, should slip through — as if it were a PTA meeting, and Paul waiting at home! Even in crisis, it seemed, the old hungers persisted.

To the commonplaces of Pamela's life, nostalgia now lent a veneer of preciousness. Even around her unhappiness, her chronic dissatisfactions, a halo of sentimental fondness formed. For at least in those days there had been someone to come home to.

It was at this desolated moment that she felt the tap on her shoulder and, turning, found herself face to face with the woman in green, the one who had been staring at her.

"I have to introduce myself," the woman said. "This is very weird. I almost couldn't believe it myself. And maybe you'll slug me, but that's the risk I've got to take because here, at least, we're all in the same boat, aren't we?"

The woman smiled. Her teeth were a little crooked; stained from smoking.

"What are you talking about?" Pamela asked.

"I'm Muriel," the woman said. "Muriel Peete."

Pamela stepped back. "But I —"

"Don't blame Diane. She has no idea. Why should she? As far as she's concerned I'm just Muriel, which isn't that common a name but enough of one, and anyway, until tonight I had no idea you and she were friends. Of course I recognized you the minute you walked in the door. There are pictures in Kelso's wallet. I looked at them, I admit it. I was curious. I thought you were so pretty!" She smiled again, free from self-consciousness, despite her teeth. "I suppose you recognized me too —"

"No! Why should I have?"

"I assumed — but I guess not. I guess there's no reason you would have." Muriel swayed from one foot to the other. "Well, it just goes to show you. Anyway, I realize you probably don't want to talk to me. I feel horrible about what happened, really, Pamela. May I call you Pamela? Only Kelso says you're doing better now —"

"Not really."

"Oh. You're not?"

"No, things are pretty terrible." She looked her rival in the eye. Such an ugly woman, finally! It was almost gratifying: as if what Kelso was saying wasn't, You're not good enough, but rather, You're too good. I need someone lower, on my own level.

For a few seconds they were silent. Then Muriel said, "Okay, I guess that's it. Anyway, before I go off and stick my head in the sand, I just want to say, you should count yourself lucky. Your boy sounds like at least he's leading a steady life. Whereas my Stewart, when he came home for Christmas, he had this big sore on his lip — and what are you supposed to say to something like that? I ask you. What are you supposed to do? I could barely eat the Christmas turkey, thinking how he got it, who gave it to him." She shook her head. "Well, that's all. Good-bye, Pamela. You don't have to shake my hand. I'm glad to know you, I hope one day . . . no, that's asking too much. Good-bye."

She left. To her surprise, Pamela found she was still standing in exactly the same spot where she'd been interrupted. In her hand the same plate on which someone else's not very good brownie, too dry, was breaking up.

All at once she was glad she'd taken the trouble to dress up, wished only that she *had* gotten a haircut.

"Well, what did you think?" Diane asked, coming up to her. "Was the meeting good for you?"

"Oh, fine. Still, that poor woman I was talking to just now, with the teeth" — she pointed in Muriel's direction — "I must say, I do feel sorry for her. It sounds like her son's really promiscuous!"

Diane smiled feebly, as across her own cheerful face, a tiny tremor passed. Then she said very primly, "Promiscuous is a word we don't use. It's judgmental."

She moved on.

Surreptitiously dashing the bad brownie into the trash, Pamela served herself up two of her own lemon nut bars.

*All in the same boat indeed.*

She wiped crumbs from her lips. *I'll get rid of that tree tonight,* she decided, then, saying a fast good-bye to Diane,

hurried out to her car and drove home. It was eight-thirty —
eleven-thirty in New York. Too late to call? No matter. They
were young.

In the kitchen, before she'd even taken off her coat, she
picked up the phone and dialed Paul's number.

Three rings.

"Hello?"

"Is this Teddy?"

"No, Teddy's not home."

"Who is it then?"

"Bobby. Teddy's friend."

"Oh, I see. Hello, Bobby. This is Paul's mother, Mrs.
Porterfield."

"Oh, hi!"

"I gather Paul's not there."

"No, he's —"

"Practicing. I know. Listen, could you tell him I — no, on
second thought, I'll try him back."

"No problem, Mrs. Porterfield."

"Thanks, Bobby. Bye."

She hung up. Of course she had the other number, too.
Kennington's number. She'd copied it from Paul's address
book. And yet would a phone call really be adequate?

Terrible, terrible: to lead a woman on like that, to keep her
guessing. And the whole time he was . . .

She moved toward the bedroom. A delicious feeling came
over her: it was power. For now she could rescue Paul, and

even though he would be furious on the surface, underneath, she knew, he would be afraid. And she would let him stay afraid. She wouldn't tell him he was once again a boon to her. She wouldn't tell him about the woman in green, moving even now across a landscape of uncertainty to her lover of the Summit Motor Lodge, and her son of the scarlet sore.

# THE HAND THAT FEEDS YOU

# 17

KENNINGTON AND JOSEPH were trying to make love. In that commodious bed where he had slept with Paul Porterfield a week before, Joseph rooted around on top of his lover, licking at his chest until the hairs got stuck in his teeth. Under him Kennington squirmed, grimaced.

"Ouch! Not so hard!"

"Sorry."

"And slide down, all your weight's on my stomach."

"Is that better?"

"Yes."

Joseph licked Kennington's balls. Silence.

"Are you all right?" he asked after a moment.

"Fine. Just tired. I didn't sleep much on the plane."

"Why don't you take a little nap, then?"

"But you know that's the worst thing for jet lag."

"Don't worry, I'll wake you before too long."

He climbed off. Turning on his side, Kennington pulled the bedspread to his neck. "Are you still horny?" he asked after a moment.

"Some."

"Why don't you watch a video?"

"Ssh. Rest. The last thing you need is to have to listen to the television."

"But it wouldn't bother me."

"Don't worry. I'm tired too. I'll rest too."

Kennington closed his eyes. Through the drawn blinds the sun turned orange. A silence peculiar to Sunday afternoons in winter gathered round him, soft with the woolly gratification of arrival. Then a creaking noise interrupted his reverie. With excruciating slowness the bedside drawer was being inched open. Farther and farther it emerged, wood abrading wood, until it yanked the phone off the table. Joseph cursed; replaced the phone; opened the lotion bottle, which, being nearly empty, made farting noises as he shook it over his palm.

After a few minutes there was a grunt. Joseph got up. From the bedroom, Kennington heard the sink run, the toilet flush.

He was gone by the time Joseph came out again. Wondering what had become of him, Joseph put on his robe and followed a trail of light to the kitchen, where he found his friend examining some garlic he'd taken out of the pantry.

"What are you doing?"

"Making dinner."

"But I thought you wanted to nap."

"I changed my mind." He opened the refrigerator. "You got anything in this icebox of yours?" he asked, his voice going high in imitation of Butterfly McQueen. "But really, this refrigerator is a disgrace. I mean, look at this butter. It expired last year! And what's this, pray tell?"

He plucked a desiccated carrot from the vegetable bin.

"Sorry," Joseph said. "When you're away, I don't always —"

"Never mind. I can still make a simple spaghetti."

Kennington pulled a cutting board out of a drawer and started to peel the cloves.

"I guess I must have woken you," Joseph said, sitting down on a stool.

"You have a habit of making more noise when you mean to make less."

"I do. I know I do."

"So much so that sometimes I can't help but wonder if you're trying to get my attention."

"Why should I want to get your attention?"

"You tell me."

"I didn't know that I *did*." Joseph could be willfully obtuse when he chose. "By the by, did I tell you what happened with Bernice?"

"No."

"Well, you remember that after she retired, I kept waiting for the go-ahead to hire a new secretary? So yesterday morning, finally, I get this memo from personnel telling me that due to 'budgetary downsizing' — that was the phrase they used — they've decided that instead of hiring someone new I should share with Peggy. Me, share a secretary!"

"So?"

"So! The point is, it's not really about downsizing, just like that business with the phone bills wasn't really about cutting back on expenses. It's a way of saying, 'You're not the big shot you think you are.' As if I couldn't get a job anywhere in town just by making a phone call."

Kennington started chopping the garlic. "Maybe I'm naïve," he said, "but I'd be more inclined to take them at their word. Everyone's tightening their belts these days."

"Be careful! You nearly sliced your thumb off."

"The knife was nowhere near my thumb." Brushing the garlic peels onto his palm, Kennington tossed them in the trash. "Are you ever going to get a garbage disposal put in? I keep telling you to."

"You know they're illegal in New York."

"So? You can still get them. I got one."

"Oh, I am so tired of this!" Joseph clapped his hand against his forehead. "It's the same old trick you've been playing for years. Instead of telling me you're upset, you pretend everything's hunky-dory, and then you stick your hand into a garbage disposal, or threaten to whack it off with a knife, or —"

"But I'm only chopping garlic!"

"Why don't you just admit you're pissed off because I woke you up? Then we'll have something to talk about."

"I would if I were, but I'm not."

Joseph shook his head. "I have to be honest. I don't know how much longer I can take this."

"No one's making you take anything." Kennington put the knife down. "Christ, do we have to have a psychodrama every time I walk into a kitchen and start to cook?"

"I'm sorry. I'm probably tired."

"You're tired! I'm the one who just got off a plane from Tokyo."

"Look, let's just pretend this conversation didn't happen, all right? Turn back the clock."

Sighing loudly, Kennington returned to chopping the garlic.

"I love you," Joseph said after a moment.

There was no reply.

"Aren't you going to answer me?"

"No."

"Why?"

"Because you're only saying it so that I'll say it back. So that I'll reassure you."

"No I'm not. I'm saying it because . . . oh, never mind. Call me when dinner's ready, will you?"

"I will."

Joseph left, the door swishing shut behind him.

# 18

TUSHI STRAUSS had been married three times to three famous conductors, by each of whom she had a son. The two older boys, now twenty and seventeen respectively, lived in England, where one studied at Cambridge and the other at Eton. The third, who was thirteen and called Nicky, lived in New York with his mother. A sullen child, he spent most of his time in his room, listening to Pearl Jam CDs, picking his pimples (which his mother tried to stop him from doing), and smoking pot (which his mother didn't know he did). He remained on bad terms with her young man, whom he seemed unable to perceive other than through a scrim of apprehension and ill-concealed loathing, no matter how often the young man offered to take him to the zoo, or play ball with him, or go to the movies with him. Indeed, the only person in Tushi's circle whom he seemed genuinely to like was Kennington. And Kennington, though he couldn't explain exactly why, liked Nicky back. Perhaps it was because something in the boy's ugly duckling constitution spoke to a similar strain in his own. Nor did it matter that at thirteen Kennington had been playing Chopin études. The identification took place below the level of achievement. It was a matter of soul, of how they addressed the world. So every couple of Saturdays, if he was in town, Kennington would head over to Tushi's apartment on East End Avenue, pick Nicky up, and take him out for some sort of treat. Nicky always got to choose. Usually he wanted to eat Chinese food, of which he was preternaturally fond, then go to the movies — ideally an action movie. And Kennington, especially if he was just back from a tour, enjoyed the movies as much as Nicky did. They seemed to offer a tonic to the cerebral labor of performance. Toward mayhem — villains exploding, planes crashing — the two of them would incline their faces for an hour and a half, much in the same way that a child inclines his face out the open window of a fast-moving car, letting the wind tug his hair back to the roots. Then Kennington would buy Nicky an ice cream cone, and take him home. "Did you like the movie?" he'd always ask, and Nicky, in his glum fashion, would always answer, "It was okay" — as if to admit even the slightest pleasure would be to violate a principle or ethic. "Thank you," he'd conclude when they got back to the apartment, before shaking Kennington's hand and retreating once again to his fetid room. And Tushi, too, would say thank you, and make tea. They would talk. Kennington enjoyed these talks at least as much as he enjoyed the movies. No matter the season, Tushi's apartment lay muffled in a cottony gauze of languor that the absence of her young man, this particular afternoon, served only to deepen.

Tushi looked good these days. Because her complexion was pale and her hair dark, at unhappy moments she tended (as did he) toward pastiness. Being in love, however, had put color in her cheeks, color that her signature black leotard and skirt only accentuated. When she was suffering, the same black leotard and skirt played horribly off her white skin, making her look like a statue of Brescian marble.

Pulling her hair back over her shoulder, she poured tea. "So I've been meaning to tell you something," she said. "You'll never guess who I ran into just before Christmas. That well-dressed page turner from San Francisco. Do you remember?"

Kennington, who was eating a cookie, stopped in midbite.

"Yes, I remember," he said.

"Actually, at the time I didn't recognize him. I mean, I recognized his face, I just couldn't place it. Then a few weeks later I couldn't sleep, and it flashed on me. He must be at Juilliard."

"Where did you see him?"

"At Joseph's. Remember when you were in Japan, he hosted that recital in his apartment, the one where I played with the Vietnamese boy?"

"He said something about it. Only what was Paul doing there?"

"Is that his name? Paul?"

"I think so. I think it was Paul."

"Well, he was turning the pages, of course." Tushi laughed. "A funny boy. Very formal and stiff and yet at the same time . . . I'm not sure quite how to put it. Tragic, sort of."

"What did Joseph say?"

"I haven't talked to him about it. I only remembered last night."

Taking another cookie, Kennington crossed, then recrossed his legs.

"Speaking of Joseph," Tushi went on, "how are things going between you two these days?"

"Why should they be going any differently than they usually do?"

"Well, Richard" — she played with her ankh — "you know as well as I do that when you were in Rome, he was upset, to put it mildly."

"Did he tell you that?"

"Only that there was some sort of communications problem. Once you got back, I assumed you'd worked it out, since he didn't say anything more."

"Yes, we're okay. He's okay." Kennington put down his cup. "I guess the truth is that we get along best when I'm out of town a lot, so I just . . . arrange to be out of town a lot."

"But I thought you hated traveling."

"I do. More than ever my dream is only to make records."

"Then why don't you? You could afford it."

"Because if I did, Joseph and I would be on top of each other all the time. Also, he wouldn't have enough to do."

"Of course he would. He has other clients."

"But we grew up together. We made our reputations together. If I quit . . . it would feel too much like the end of something, wouldn't it? For Joseph especially."

Tushi, silent, stared into her tea leaves.

"Is something wrong?" he asked.

"Richard, forgive me if in asking this I'm overstepping my

bounds, but is the thing you really hate so much going on concert tours, or being with Joseph?"

"Tushi! That's a terrible thing to say. I love Joseph."

"I know you do. Even so, I can't help but notice that for all your talk of wanting to quit, you always find some excuse not to. It's as if being away is the lesser of two evils."

"But I told you, it would hurt Joseph too much. Also, he's not as young as he used to be, he doesn't have the kind of clout he used to have at the agency. Without me —"

"He's just taken on that Vietnamese boy, hasn't he?"

"Why are you giving me the third degree?"

"Because what you're saying isn't consistent. I mean, I believe you when you say you're afraid of hurting him. But, Richard, don't you see that you're hurting him a whole lot more right now, being on the road all the time and having affairs and —"

"So what are you suggesting? That we give up our — how shall I put it — extracurricular activities and become your average monogamous couple? I mean, when I'm on tour Joseph isn't exactly sitting at home making jam, Tushi —"

"I'm not saying that he is. I'm simply saying that maybe it's time to think about moving forward."

"But I could never leave Joseph."

"No, I don't believe you could. And yet you could make things so intolerable for him that eventually he'd have no choice but to leave you. And if that's your plan, you've got to give it up. It's childish."

Kennington put down his cup in annoyance. "Oh, I am so

tired of being told I'm childish: 'the little prodigy who never grew up, the little boy who never grew up.'"

"But you haven't, in certain ways. And you can't blame Joseph, either."

"Why not? If I still think of myself as a boy, it's his doing. For instance, he used to call me 'son' — when we were in bed." Kennington glowered. "I wasn't much older than Nicky at the time. Does that surprise you?"

"No."

"Fifteen years old, and Joseph leaning over me and saying, 'Now I'm going to fuck you, son. Are you ready to get fucked by your daddy?'"

"Richard —"

"I made him do it. He didn't want to, at first. But once he started, you can't imagine how excited he got, how excited we both got —"

"Please keep your voice down," Tushi said, gesturing toward Nicky's door.

"Oh, the child! Forgive me if I should offend the child's tender ears!"

Tushi was silent. Across from her, Kennington moved his fingers through his hair with tourettic intensity.

"Well, there you have it," he said after a few moments. "The lurid detail, always guessed at, never discussed."

"Richard, it's not —"

"And now I have something to ask you. That boy, that page turner. Why did you really tell me about him? Was it because Joseph put you up to it?"

"No, of course not. Why would he have?"

"Because . . ." A beat of silence passed. "Well, Joseph can be jealous. Maybe he wondered if in San Francisco —"

"As I told you, Joseph and I have never discussed that boy."

"I guess I have a suspicious mind." Kennington stood. "Listen, I'd better be going. I've got to —" He broke off the sentence. "You know what my real problem is, Tushi? It's that it's so easy to pretend you're doing something to save someone else, when really you're only doing it to save yourself."

"Richard —"

He held out his hand, as if to block her. "It's all right. Please don't say anything. I've told you too much already."

"What have you told me that I didn't already know?"

"I'm afraid I really have to go. I promised I'd be back by seven."

She brushed back his hair. "I'm worried about you. Both of you."

"Well, don't worry. Even if I'm a boy, I'm a big boy. Thanks for the tea."

They kissed, and she walked him to the door, where he turned. "Oh, I've been meaning to ask you," he said. "Something someone asked me once. If your hands were cut off and put in a lineup, would you recognize them?"

She laughed. "What a strange question!" And she looked at her hands. "You mean without the rings, or anything?"

"Yes, just your hands."

"I'm not sure," Tushi said. "Would you?"

"I'm sure I wouldn't. Well, I'd better be going. Tell Nicky good-bye for me."

He left. She shut the door behind him. It was nearly sunset, and the curtains were blowing out an open window in her kitchen. She went to close it, and as she did, leaned out to watch Kennington leave. He was running across East End Avenue, waving and shouting at a cab. Then the cab stopped. He got in.

Off he rode, into swarms of yellow and red.

For warmth, she squeezed her own arms, which prickled, and shut the window firmly. Odd: suddenly the apartment seemed so full of shadows that she became frightened and, running through the corridors, switched on every lamp, every fixture. Next she put on music, Saint-Saëns's *Carnival of the Animals,* the most innocent thing she could think of. And still she felt frightened.

Finally she did something she almost never did. She knocked on Nicky's door.

"Who is it?"

"It's Mom. Can I come in?"

"Just a second." Shufflings sounded, a bolt was released. "Okay."

In darkness Nicky sat on his futon. He had the curtains tightly drawn. From the earphones of his Walkman a bleat of music thumped, tinny and whining.

"Hello, darling," Tushi said, and, throwing herself down on the futon, took him roughly in her arms.

"Mom, stop!"

"I love you, Nicky. I hope you know that."

"Mom, please."

She held him. Soon he stopped protesting and closed his eyes. Pressing her teeth into the hard silkiness of his shoulder, she put on her best Transylvanian accent, and said, "I am a vampire. I am going to suck your blood."

"Oh, right."

"Mmm, fresh boy blood. Delicious."

"You *are* a vampire." He laughed.

"I wish I could drink *you!*" she said, and wished, suddenly, for her other boys as well; also, for the first time, that the young man might not come back tonight, so that she could spend this evening alone with Nicky.

Curious: when she'd first met him, she'd thought of Kennington in the same way that she now thought of the young man; had imagined seducing him, marrying him. Until she'd learned which choir he sang in.

Where was he now? Halfway across town, probably, nearly to the apartment where Joseph waited for him, just as he had waited every day, these many years. He had patience, Joseph. She did not. That was why her own history, for all its small misfortunes, would never amount to a tragedy.

At length she let Nicky go. Rubbing his arms, he rolled away from her.

"Did Richard take you for Chinese lunch?" she asked.

"Yes."

"And are you so sick of Chinese food that you couldn't eat it for dinner?"

Nicky hesitated. "I guess I could handle it," he answered after a second's contemplation.

"Come on, then," she said, "we're going out," and stepping into the bathroom, she had to shield her eyes against the halogen bulbs. In the mirror an aging woman looked back at her: a woman with a lover young enough to be her son.

"It's okay," she said to no one. But was it? And, remembering, for some reason, the page turner, she put on her favorite lipstick, her spiciest perfume.

With her hands. *Her* hands.

Bulging veins, blunt nails, age spots.

"Ready?" she shouted, shutting the bathroom door behind her.

"Ready," Nicky answered sullenly.

"Come on, then." And bundling an arm around him, she herded him toward the elevator.

When Kennington arrived ten minutes later, Joseph was on his knees in the living room, rifling through some old programs and photographs that he'd pulled from a bureau drawer.

"What are you looking for?" Kennington asked as he shut the door.

"Well, it's the damnedest thing. One of the photographs is missing from the bookcase."

"Which one?"

"The one of you at the Trevi Fountain."

"Are you sure you didn't move it?"

"I've looked everywhere."

Kennington took off his coat. "I wonder what could have happened to it," he said, sitting down and picking up the Game Boy.

"All I can think is that Maria must have broken it while she was dusting. She's done that before, broken things, then hidden them so I wouldn't find out."

"And you think she hid it in that drawer?"

"That's where she put that porcelain dog she broke last year. And you have to start somewhere . . . oh, look at this." He opened a yellowing pamphlet. "You know what this is? The program from that concert you played in Dallas, when you were fifteen."

"If you're wondering whether Maria broke the frame, why don't you just ask her?"

"Oh, and here's another one. From Rome, the same trip when I took the picture."

"Look, are we going to dinner or aren't we?"

"We are. I just thought I'd see if I could find the picture first."

"But isn't that like looking for a needle in a haystack? And anyway, who knows whether Maria broke it? Maybe someone stole it."

"Why would anyone want to steal it? It didn't have a silver frame. And there are plenty of things in the apartment that are much more valuable." Joseph hauled himself up from the floor. "Still, you're right, it is like looking for a needle in a haystack." He brushed off his trousers. "Well, are you ready?"

Kennington didn't hear him. He was holding his hands in front of his eyes and staring at them, almost as if he were trying to memorize something.

"Richard?"

"What?" He put his hands down. "Sorry. Yes, I'm ready."

And they went to dinner.

# 19

SHE FLEW ALL DAY, on a flight she could not actually afford, to a city she had visited only once, on her honeymoon (irony of ironies), long ago and in another life. The roads were sleety, which only intensified the ordinary end-of-day traffic. Nor did the taxi driver, a heavyset, unsmiling Jamaican named Desmond Fairclough, provide much in the way of reassurance. Would he kidnap her, she wondered, rape and maim her in some South Bronx lot? Already she could see the broken glass, the audience of hooters. Or perhaps Desmond Fairclough planned only to cheat her, to take her on some ridiculously roundabout route in order to inflate the already excessive fare. It was possible. She had no idea where she was, other than in a whorl of wetness and clashing light. Not for the first time, her life was in a stranger's hands.

Then they crossed a bridge, and crossed an avenue, and another avenue. "White Street," Desmond Fairclough announced, sooner than she'd expected, and opened the door. She stepped outside. He helped her hoist her suitcase from the trunk, took her money, and veered off into the weather. The street was empty, eerily quiet. Loading docks lunged over the sidewalks. Across the way, a sign advertised something called the Wing Fat Fish Company. All of this alarmed her. After all, she had assumed that Kennington would live in a good neighborhood, an opulent neighborhood, in a gracious skyscraper from the lobby of which doormen would flock to usher her in. Instead she found herself amid fish factories and the odor of raw meat. Was it possible there were two White Streets in Manhattan? Or maybe the driver had misunderstood her instructions, and she wasn't in Manhattan at all. Death felt, suddenly, imminent, close at hand.

Still, she had to see. So she gathered up her suitcase and, hobbling over to the building marked 48, rang the intercom.

After a few seconds a male voice answered.

"Richard?"

Crashing noises in the background. "I can't hear you!"

"Richard Kennington?"

A buzzer sounded; the door unlatched itself. Pushing through, Pamela made her way to the elevator, which turned out to be a freight model: entirely too big for her and her single Samsonite. Up she rode, to the third floor, where the elevator opened onto a narrow foyer. Across the way a steel door hung ajar, music sounding through the crack: classical music. So perhaps she had come to the right place after all.

She stepped inside. The apartment was huge, the floor a sea of yellow wood planks stretching to windows that towered seven or eight feet over the street. Buckling pine bookshelves lined the walls. Near the center of the room a small crowd was milling around a grand piano, while on the coffee table, a platter of dip and vegetables sat ravaged, picked through. *So he's having a party,* she thought. Somehow it hadn't occurred to her that he might be having a party. And meanwhile no one was paying her the least attention. Nor did she recognize Paul, or Kennington himself, for that matter, among the assembled luminaries, in the haze of smoke and chatter.

Eventually a woman with long black hair detached herself from the crowd around the piano and slunk over to greet Pamela, who stood cowering in her raincoat, suitcase between her legs. "Hello," she said, holding out a long hand. "Can I take your bag?"

"I'm looking for Richard Kennington," Pamela said. "Have I come to the right apartment?"

"Of course. Richard should be back any minute now. You see, he's flying in from Chicago tonight, but with the weather being so bad, his flight was delayed." Tushi peered cryptically at the suitcase. "Can *I* help you with anything?"

"I'm here for my son" was Pamela's frosty reply.

"Your son. But who is your son?"

"*You* should know."

"I'm sorry, I don't —"

"From the concert, if nothing else. The one in San Francisco. But there's no point in any of this because I know he's here. There's no use pretending."

"Mrs. —"

"Porterfield."

Pamela scanned the room anxiously.

"Mrs. Porterfield, I'm sorry to disappoint you, but I don't think your son *is* here, actually. What did you say his name was?"

"Paul."

A young man wearing an apron drifted in from the kitchen. "Can I help you with something, darling?" he asked, wrapping his arm around Tushi's waist.

"No, everything's fine. We've just got a little confusion here. You see, Mrs. Porterfield is looking for her son Paul, whom she's convinced is at the party. Only I've never heard of him."

"Well, there's one way to find out." And forming his hands into a bullhorn, the young man called out: "Your attention please. Paul Porterfield. Paging Paul Porterfield. Is there a Paul Porterfield in the house?"

All at once Joseph separated himself from the crowd and hurried over to Pamela, who had now settled down on top of her suitcase and was crying quietly.

"What's this about Paul Porterfield?" he asked. "Who's looking for him?"

"I am," Pamela answered meekly. "I'm his mother."

"But why . . ."

Behind them the door swung open. Kennington, bearing his own suitcase, walked in.

Pamela stood.

"Surprise," the guests shouted, before breaking into a hearty rendition of "Happy Birthday."

Very stiffly Kennington put down the suitcase.

"Where is Paul?" Pamela asked, her voice cold. "You can't hide him from me."

"But I don't —"

"You can't hide him from me," she repeated.

"I don't intend to hide him from you," Kennington said. "I have no idea where Paul is. I haven't seen him since Rome."

"Rome?" Joseph asked.

"I think maybe you three ought to talk in here," Tushi said, very efficiently moving across the floor to hold the bedroom door open for them.

There was no place to sit. The bed was covered with coats. So they stood, all three of them in postures of discomfort, Pamela pulling at her fingers, Kennington and Joseph leaning against the window, their arms wrapped tightly over their chests.

"Where is Paul?" Pamela once again demanded. "I want my son. I've come to get my son."

"I'm sorry, but I don't have any idea."

"Don't lie to me. Especially after Rome —"

"What is this about Rome?" Joseph thrust in. "Richard, how on earth do you know this woman?"

"We met when I was there in June. Just by chance."

"And who are *you*?" Pamela interrupted. "How do *you* know my son?"

"I'm Mr. Kennington's agent. And I only know Paul because before Christmas I ran into him in the elevator in my building. I —"

"What was he doing in your building?"

"He has a friend downstairs from me. And he remembered me from San Francisco, and we got to talking. Later I asked him if he'd like to turn pages at a little recital I was hosting. This was when you were in Japan," he added to Kennington.

"Why didn't you tell me this?"

"What was the point? I didn't know you'd met these people in Rome."

"I don't see why you're bothering with all these lies. It's no use," Pamela said, sitting down on the coats.

"Mrs. Porterfield, Pamela, I'm telling you the truth. I honestly haven't seen Paul since June."

"And I'm telling you I know you're lying. I found your address in his address book. I saw the picture."

"What picture?"

"The one you gave him. The one you signed to him."

"But I never gave him any picture! This is insane!"

"You're wasting your time. I *saw* it."

"Well, maybe he bought a picture somewhere. Sometimes I sign them after concerts —"

"*That* picture? I don't think so."

"What was the picture?" inquired Joseph.

"It was of him in Rome. At the Trevi Fountain. No doubt you got a kick out of my humiliation that night."

Joseph turned, gazed at Kennington, who sat next to Pamela on the bed.

A hush descended.

"There's a party going on," Kennington said presently. "We can't stay in here all night."

"Yes," Pamela said. "Far be it for a mother to get in the way of some highbrow party. But you needn't worry because I didn't come here to spoil your fun. I came here for Paul. And so if you'd just be kind enough to tell me where I might locate him —"

"Pamela —"

"Have you tried his apartment?" Joseph suggested.

She shook her head. "He's never there. He's always practicing. He *claims.*"

"It's at least worth giving a call." Kennington handed her the telephone.

Reluctantly she accepted it, dialed, waited.

Soon enough her expression changed.

"Hello, Teddy? This is Mrs. Porterfield. I'm fine, how are you? Good. Listen, honey, is Paul there? No, there's no message. All right, I'll call back later."

She hung up. "Any other bright ideas?"

"He might actually be practicing," Joseph said. "Or, there is one other possibility." He glanced at Pamela, who still held the phone. "May I?"

"Be my guest."

She handed it to him. He dialed 411.

"Yes, have you got a listing for an Alden Haynes, please? H-A-Y-N-E-S. On Central Park West. Thank you."

Pushing down the little buttons on the cradle of the phone, he dialed again.

"Hello, Alden? Joseph Mansourian here. Fine, fine. Yes, far too long. Listen, I'm sorry to bother you at this hour, I realize it's rather awkward, but I'm looking for that young friend of yours, Paul Porterfield. I don't know if he mentioned that we met in the elevator . . . yes. It's rather urgent that I speak to him, you see, I have his mother here, and she's been searching all over town for him . . . He is? Good, good. Thank you."

He handed the phone to Pamela, whose face had over the course of the conversation grown rather flushed.

"Hello, Paul? Hello. Darling, I'm so glad to see your voice. Hear your voice, I mean. Gosh, I'm nervous." Again, she smiled. "Well, guess what, sweetheart? I'm in New York. I'm at Richard Kennington's apartment."

"You're *where?*" Kennington heard Paul shouting.

"I'll just go and make sure everything's all right outside," Joseph said, stepping carefully over Kennington's knees and out the door.

Together, they deposited Pamela and her suitcase in a cab, then got into the elevator.

"Why didn't you tell me you'd met these people?" Joseph asked as the doors shut.

"Why should I? Is it my duty to report to you every time I meet someone?"

"No, of course not. And yet if this woman's to be taken

seriously, your involvement with her had to have been quite a bit more than just a conversation in the street. You had to have —"

"I helped her out when some gypsies tried to steal her purse. That was all."

"And the son?"

"We got to be friends. He's a fan."

"Did you sleep with him?"

"Joseph!"

"You've got to tell me. After all, I'm the one he stole from. And you have to admit, you've never been very astute at judging these sorts of situations, Richard. I mean, don't you remember San Francisco? He knew everything about you. Who's to say he didn't *arrange* to be in the elevator that day, just so that he could inveigle his way into my apartment, so that he could —"

"Joseph! You're the one who asked him to page-turn."

"Has he called you? Written you any letters?"

The doors to the elevator opened. "Darling," Tushi called, rushing from the apartment. "Is the madwoman gone?"

"She's gone," Joseph said. "We put her in a cab."

"I must tell you," she continued, clapping an arm around each of their backs, "when I first saw her, I thought she was some sort of deranged fan."

"She's not a deranged fan," Kennington said. "She's not any kind of fan at all."

"She's just an unhappy woman who wants her son," Joseph added.

"Oh, her son. I meant to ask you. Who is her son? She said something about San Francisco."

"The page turner," Joseph said. "The well-dressed page turner."

"That's her son? Oh, dear. Well, happy birthday!"

"Happy birthday!" the crowd echoed, as Tushi's young man, for the second time, carried in the cake, which was in the form of a piano.

"Make a wish!" he cried, after they'd finished singing.

Kennington did. He blew out the candles.

"Chocolate and white chocolate," Joseph said. "Your favorites."

"Yes, my favorites," Kennington repeated, and plunged the knife into the soundboard.

# 20

ALL THE OTHER GUESTS had left the party, and Tushi and her young man were dancing. They were dancing — she'd put one of Kennington's Billie Holiday CDs on the stereo — and so they did not hear the noises from the kitchen, where Joseph was helping Kennington clean up.

Kennington's kitchen, though small, was very fancy. It had Carrara marble countertops, polished birch cabinets, a Sub-Zero fridge, and Thermador ovens. It had a clever little re-volving cabinet in the corner, and pullout spice racks, and a disposal, into which Kennington was at the moment furi-ously scraping stale vegetable mousses and celery ends. Peri-odically he would switch the thing on, so that its roar might further abstract his and Joseph's conversation, already muted, for Tushi and her young man, by the voice of Billie Holiday, the scratchy sinuous tonalities of a blues band.

"I'm telling you," Joseph was saying, "you've got to call the police. To protect yourself."

"And I'm telling you there's no need."

"Are you kidding? Don't you remember what happened to that girl, that actress, in California? Or Versace, for God's sake."

"Joseph, listen to me. You are overreacting. There's no reason to think —"

"Easy for you to say, when it's my apartment he was prowling around in. And God knows what else he pawed over."

"Please give me some credit as a judge of character. Paul's not like that."

"Then why did he steal that picture?"

"I don't know. He admires me. Anyway, stealing a picture doesn't mean he's packing a revolver."

"I'm not saying it does. I'm just saying you can't be too careful these days."

Kennington thrust a bowl under the tap, scrubbed at it, put it in the dishwasher.

"I hope you realize I'm only bringing all this up because I want to protect you," Joseph went on. "Because I'm worried about you."

"Are you?"

"Why else would I make such a fuss?"

"I don't know. Maybe because you're jealous."

"Do I have reason to be jealous?"

"No."

"Good."

"Still, that hasn't stopped you before."

"Wait a minute. This isn't about jealousy. It's about the fact that clearly you became much more involved with these people than you've let on, otherwise that demented woman would never have —"

"Pamela's not demented. She's in the middle of a divorce. And anyway, she's not Paul."

"They could be working together. They could —"

"Will you keep your voice down? None of this is their fault. If it's anyone's fault, it's mine."

"So you did sleep with him. Was he underage?"

"That never stopped you."

"And what about the picture? If he was underage . . ."

"I don't know. Jesus, it's just a snapshot, Joseph. It was days before you even noticed it was missing, and now you're acting like he committed grand larceny." Kennington breathed shakily. "I'll say this one last time. Paul Porterfield is a perfectly decent, somewhat naive boy who —"

Joseph laughed. "You can really be so naive sometimes —"

"Don't talk to me like that."

"That boy really took you for a ride, didn't he? He had you thinking he was Little Mary Sunshine. Didn't it ever occur to you it might be a tactic?"

"Did it ever occur to you that not everyone in the world is out to get something?"

Joseph grimaced. "There's no way around it. I have to tell you."

"Tell me what?"

"He did it to me too."

"Did what?"

"Came on to me." Joseph hesitated, as liars are inclined to do. "Of course I knew better than to take him up on it —"

Kennington stepped back. He laughed.

"I've only kept it from you to protect you. But now we have to face facts. After he turned pages for Thang that evening, he stuck around."

"Joseph —"

"It was hard to get rid of him. And I'm sure we're not the only ones. A boy like that never barks up just one tree. Later, I saw him at a concert. I introduced him to Harry Moore. For all I know Harry might —"

"I don't want to hear this."

"You have to. You're not a child anymore. Today you're forty. You've got to accept that people will try to use you."

"Do you have to be so loud?" Hurrying toward the sink, Kennington switched on the disposal.

"Oh, so it's going to be that again, is it?" Joseph yelled over the noise. "The disposal game?"

"No."

"You're too old for that now. Too old —"

"Please shut up. Can't you shut up?"

Joseph was silent. Crossing the room very calmly, he switched off the disposal, so that once again the voice of Billie Holiday penetrated into the kitchen.

> Oh my man I love him so,
> he'll never know
> all my life is just despair
> but I don't care . . .

In the living room, Tushi leaned her head into the young man's shoulder. "I hope they're all right," she said.

"I'm sure there's nothing to worry about," he answered, nuzzling her ear.

Again, the disposal switched on.

*Nothing to worry about,* Tushi repeated to herself.

And they continued dancing.

# 21

THE TAXI had dropped Pamela off, and she was once again alone on a sidewalk, in a neighborhood — if this was possible — even more sinister than Kennington's. Dirty buildings rose up around her, the bricks gaudy under yellow streetlamps. A homeless woman, wrapped in cardboard and blankets, lay asleep on Paul's stoop, while near the corner several boys, their jeans drooping at the buttocks, stared at her, legs restless as they shuffled amid the dirty snow heaps. One of them held a boom box from which dance music pulsed like a faint and harrowing heartbeat.

They were staring at her, not so much malevolently as assessingly, which was perhaps worse.

Picking up her suitcase, she stepped carefully over the sleeping pile of blankets and rang Paul's bell. Instantly the door clicked open, for which she was grateful; just as quickly she let herself through and shut it behind her, causing the glass pane to rattle so loudly she feared it might break. But it didn't. Safe, for the moment, she breathed. The corridor was narrow, lit by a popover-shaped lighting fixture inside of which several insect corpses reclined. The walls smelled of smoke, of unwashed hair.

Footsteps sounded overhead. She could hear the loud trip-
ping of boyish feet taking the stairs three at a time. Then two
faces were laughing in front of hers. One of them she recog-
nized as belonging to Teddy Moss. The other reminded her,
inexplicably, of a chipmunk.

"Teddy!" she cried in relief, and kissed him. "Oh, it's so
good to see you, sweetheart!"

"Good to see you too, Mrs. Porterfield. This is my friend,
Bobby Newman."

"Pleased to meet you, Bobby."

"Likewise, I'm sure."

"Well, shall we? I'm afraid there's no elevator."

"That's all right, I'm strong."

"Let me take your suitcase," Bobby said as they started
climbing. "That's a pretty perfume. Wait, let me guess. L'Air
du Temps, right?"

"In fact it is. My, you've got a good nose."

"I know my fragrances," Bobby said. "Especially the clas-
sics. I always prefer the classics. For instance, have you tried
the new Chanel? Allure? My feeling is that it's too —"

"Bobby," Teddy said, "I don't think Mrs. Porterfield wants
to talk about perfume right now."

"Actually, I don't mind."

They had reached the third landing, where Bobby put
down the suitcase.

"My, this is bracing," Pamela said. "How many more floors
do we have to go?"

"Only three. Paul's not here yet, though we expect him any minute."

"Teddy, I hope I'm not making trouble for you all, showing up like this."

"It's no trouble."

"I'm glad. I just hope that Paul won't . . . well, you know, it probably does cramp a young man's style, having his mother just appear out of the blue."

"Here we are," Teddy said, unlatching the door. "I'm afraid it's nothing splendid. Still, it's home."

"Oh, it's . . . lovely," Pamela said. The apartment, from what she could see, consisted of a long corridor off of which several rooms opened. The first of these, to which the door was closed, was Teddy's bedroom, he explained. The second was the kitchen. The third was the living room, which Paul's bedroom adjoined. The fourth was the bathroom.

"And speaking of the bathroom, might I —"

"Of course." Bobby opened the door for her.

"Thanks." She stepped inside. It was the tiniest bathroom she'd ever been in, with a sink the size of a piece of stationery. Rough lengths of Scotch tape framed a yellowing patch on the wall, as if a poster had just been taken down. What might it have depicted?

Having peed and fixed her make-up, Pamela rejoined Bobby and Teddy in the living room. This was a square about ten by ten, furnished with a sofa draped in Indian bedspreads, a large television, and several plywood bookcases.

Three windows lined the far wall, all locked and grated, looking out onto a fire escape across the way from which, in another living room, a fat girl was watching *I Love Lucy* and smoking.

"Well, this certainly is a far cry from Menlo Park," Pamela said, sitting down.

"Mrs. Porterfield," Teddy said, "I hope you won't mind my asking you this, but if you happen to speak to my mother, would you try not to worry her too much? About the apartment, I mean. She's never been to New York, so she has no idea how little a thousand dollars a month gets you."

"You pay a thousand dollars a month for this?" Pamela hadn't known, as it was Kelso who paid Paul's half of the rent.

"That's a bargain for two bedrooms," Bobby threw in. "Would you like some herbal tea, Mrs. Porterfield? Fruit juice? Water?"

"No thanks." She crossed her legs. "I hope Paul's all right."

"I'm sure he's fine. In fact" — Teddy cocked his ear — "I suspect that's him now."

Indeed, the door was unbolting. Pamela stood.

A few seconds later Paul walked in, looking flustered and pale.

"Hi, Paul."

"Hi, Teddy."

Bobby coughed significantly.

"Oh, Paul, this is Bobby. I guess you two haven't met."

"A pleasure," Bobby said, taking Paul's hand.

"A pleasure," Paul repeated.

He did not look at his mother.

"Paul?" she said after a second.

"Teddy, would you and Bobby mind leaving my mother and me alone for a little while?"

"Of course not. In fact, we were just on our way out."

"We're going to Coney Island tonight," Bobby added.

"Have fun, boys. Be safe."

Gathering up their coats, they left.

"You boys certainly do keep late hours," Pamela remarked, sitting down again.

"What are you doing here?"

"That's no way to talk —"

"I asked you a question. What are you doing here?"

"I decided I wanted to see my son. Is there anything wrong with that?"

"So you got on a plane, flew to New York, and went to Kennington's apartment? To see me?"

"You're never home."

"Christ, Mother, what were you thinking, just showing up there? How did you even get his address?"

"Never mind how I got his address." She took a tissue from her purse. "We need to talk, Paul."

"All right, what? And I hope you don't think I'm staying all night. As it happens I was in the middle of a very enjoyable dinner party when you called, and it's my full intention to be back at it within half an hour. So you'd better start, because according to my calculations you've only got" — he checked his watch — "twenty-two minutes."

"Oh, Paul, for God's sake."

Again, he looked at his watch.

"Aren't you going to sit down, at least? Aren't you going to take off your coat?"

"You've just wasted another minute."

"Paul, I can't believe you're treating me —" She arched her back. "Oh, all right, have it your way. I'm here because I know what's going on between you and that man, and I've come to put a stop to it."

"What man?"

"Don't pretend with me. You know who I'm talking about."

"No, I don't."

She pushed back her hair. "All right, if I have to spell it out for you, I will. Richard Kennington. I know what's going on between you and Richard Kennington."

"But nothing's going on between me and Richard Kennington."

"I may not be a woman of the world, honey, but I'm not naive. And you don't live half your life within spitting distance of San Francisco without becoming aware of . . . homosexuals."

"Oh, Jesus —"

"I mean, probably I should have seen the signs from the beginning, you know, that he wasn't married, that he knew all about clothes and hairdressers. Only I suppose, well, I suppose I didn't want to. I was so unhappy myself, after your father left, that I preferred to believe . . . And he took advantage of it. He took advantage of both of us."

"Christ." Sitting down, Paul cupped his head in his hands.

"I didn't really put two and two together until Christmas, when you —"

"You have misunderstood everything, again. It's your goddamned French exam, again."

"How? What have I misunderstood?"

He looked up. "I haven't seen Richard since Rome. I haven't even talked to Richard since Rome. Didn't he tell you that?"

"Of course he did. To protect himself."

"You assume. Assume makes an ass of you and me. *You* told me that. *You.*"

"But if you haven't seen him since Rome, where did the picture come from?"

"What picture?"

"The one you had at Christmas. The one he signed to you."

"What are you telling me, that you went through my suitcase?"

"I was terribly, terribly worried, sweetheart, after you said you were going to quit the piano. And then when I found the picture, everything suddenly made sense. That was why I went to his apartment. To get you away from him."

"Jesus, you have really fucked things up this time."

"Don't talk to me in that tone of voice, young man. I'm your mother —"

"Oh, be quiet —"

"And no matter how grown-up you may feel, the fact remains, you're eighteen years old. There are things you don't understand."

"Look, why don't you just go away? You're a walking disaster, you know that? The best thing you could do is just go home, get on with your life, and leave me alone."

"Don't say that!"

"And don't cry!"

"I can't help it. I come here to help you, and you treat me like —"

"I don't need your help. You need help."

"It's horrible, I might as well just . . . kill myself, just go over to that window and throw myself out. Then you'll be rid of me, you and your father and Richard —"

"Don't be so melodramatic."

"All I am to anyone is trouble. That's all I am to myself, even."

Standing up, Paul took off his coat and walked to the window. Through the grates, in the square realm of his neighbor's television, Lucy was struggling with a round of pizza dough.

Eventually he turned. His mother was perched like a bird on the extreme edge of the sofa.

"All right, look. I'm going to explain this once. Not because I owe it to you — I don't — but because I don't want you going home with the wrong impression."

"Thank you, Paul. I'm listening."

"First of all, that picture isn't mine. It belongs to Joseph, to Mr. Mansourian."

"But then how —"

"I stole it, all right?"

Silence, for a moment. "Why did you steal it?"

"Because I wanted it. Because I liked it. Because I was pissed off at Richard for dumping us in Rome. It was a stupid thing to do and I shouldn't have done it, but there it is. Also, Joseph never noticed, he has so many pictures of him already."

"He does?"

"And the only reason I have Richard's address and phone number is because I copied it out of Joseph's Rolodex. I've never been to Richard's apartment and I haven't talked to him. Not since Rome."

Sitting very still, Pamela removed the ring from her left index finger, twisted it several times, replaced it on her right index finger.

"And yet in Rome, something did happen between you, didn't it?" she asked after a moment.

Paul was silent.

Suddenly she stood and tried to embrace him. "Oh, I knew it! I knew it! So not only did he take advantage of your admiration for him, your reverence of him —"

"He didn't take advantage of me. Don't! I was perfectly conscious of what I was doing."

"Then why did he run away like a coward?"

"I don't know. Maybe it had nothing to do with us. He's an artist, and artists can't be held to the same standards —"

"Did he tell you that?"

"No, he did not."

"Being an artist doesn't justify lying."

"What, you wanted him to say, 'Mrs. Porterfield, I'm having an affair with your son, I hope you don't mind'?"

"No, not to me. Lying to you."

"He never lied to me."

"Then what did he tell you about that man? That Mansourian, or whatever his name is."

"Mother, Joseph is Richard's agent."

"Also."

"Also!"

He looked at her, his brow furrowed.

After a moment, he sat down. She sat next to him. He was studying with great intensity the patterns in the Indian bedspread that covered the sofa.

Then: "You didn't see it, did you?" Pamela said.

"Maybe I didn't let myself see it."

"Honey, I'm sorry. If I'd realized —"

"But it all makes perfect sense, doesn't it? An idiot could have put the pieces together."

"Not necessarily. You're young. Maybe you have to be my age before you can recognize a lie."

"But I should have. It was so obvious."

"Sweetheart, I just feel so bad, I just want to hug you . . . only I suppose . . . Oh, damn all that." And she hugged him.

He did not resist.

After a few minutes he pulled away from her. "It's late," he said. "You can sleep in my room."

"Oh, that's sweet of you, darling, but I'd just as soon find a hotel."

"At this hour?"

"Well . . . on second thought, maybe you're right. Only I refuse to throw you out of bed. I'll sleep here, on the couch."

"Don't be silly, Mother. Come on." And he led her into his room, where the shades were drawn, the writing implements tidy on the desk.

"My Paul," she said, kissing him on the forehead. "Always neat as a pin." Automatically she smoothed back his hair. "Well, I think I'll do my little ablutions now, if you don't mind. Oh, what about your dinner party?"

"It doesn't matter," Paul said. "You get ready for bed. I've got to make a call." And he went off to the kitchen to phone Alden.

By the time he was through, his mother had washed and changed. She was in her nightgown now, lying on his bed in the dark.

"The ceiling's covered with stars," she said.

"I know."

"Lie down next to me," she said, and he did. "I used to know all about astronomy. Before I met your father, that is. I had this boyfriend, Pete Carruthers, who was a stargazer, and he taught me."

"What did he teach you?"

"Well, for instance, that constellation there, that's Ursa Major. The Big Dipper. And that one over there, that's the Little Dipper. Ursa Minor. And that very bright star, do you know which one that is?"

"The North Star?"

"It's not a star at all. It's Mars."

"What's the bright spot behind it? Is that the North Star?"

"Ganymede," Pamela said. "One of the brightest moons that circles Jupiter."

"I know all about Ganymede," Paul said. "Jove carried him off to be his cupbearer."

"Did he?"

"Mmm-hmm."

They were silent. Not far off a clock ticked. And the stored-up light drained out of the stars.

Later that night, riding a Ferris wheel on Coney Island, Bobby Newman looked at Teddy Moss, and said, "I love you."

At first Teddy didn't answer. Up and up the Ferris wheel carried them, until they neared the top, where he reached for a sliver of alabaster moon. Silently he stretched his palm, opened his fingers into a sky that was all purples and mauves and ripe blue-browns — as if a moment could be lived so hard, it bruised.